WATCH OUT GIRLS. HERE SHE COMES.

Maneater

CAMBRIA HEBERT

Watch out, girls. Here she comes.

There's always that girl. She's popular, beautiful, and has everything together. The one with the perfectly teased hair, arms full of colorful (but coordinated) bangles, and expertly painted bright-pink lips.
A teacher's pet. Daddy's girl.
Everyone loves her.
Because everyone is afraid to challenge her.
Kelly Ross is that girl. She uses her powers of popularity for good… her own good.
She doesn't care who she hurts.
She always gets what she wants.
Including your man.
When she walks down the hallway in her hot-pink heels and ruffled denim miniskirt, all the boys' heads turn.
And all the girls start whispering.
Man-eater.
There hasn't been a single guy Kelly hasn't been able to chew up and spit out.
Until now.
Kelly has finally met her match. He's been there all along, and he's the exact opposite of everything you'd expect.

Get in on the lingo!
Please enjoy the popular 1980 slang terms at the top
of each chapter!
They're totally rad!

Maneater

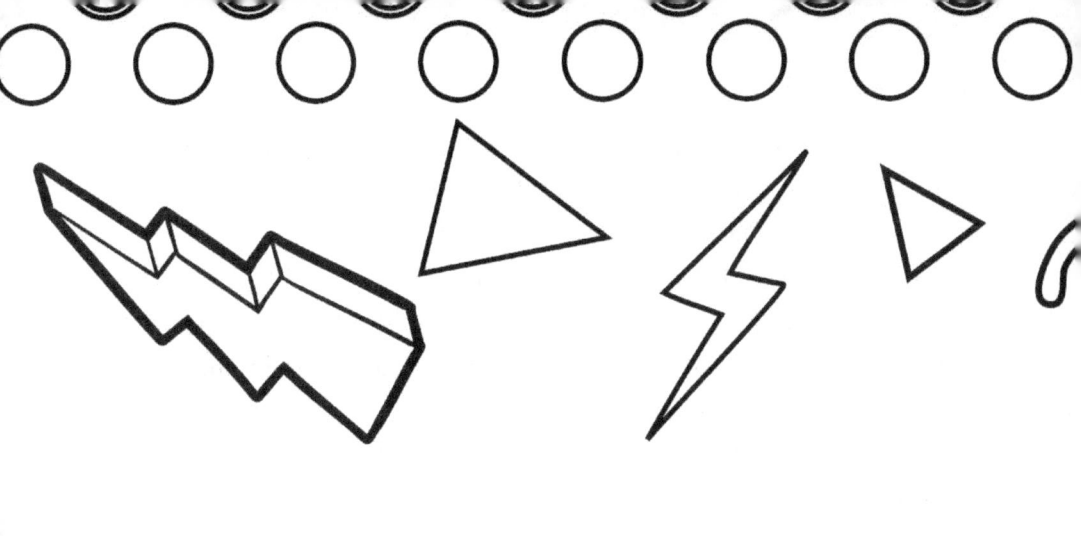

Chapter ONE

Airhead – An insult. A way to call someone stupid.

Kelly

THERE ARE TWO KINDS of people in this world. Me and everybody else.

Go ahead, roll your eyes. Think what a spoiled, egomaniac I am. I am spoiled and I do have a lot of confidence, so you wouldn't be wrong. But I'm not wrong either.

In high school everyone has roles to fill. Teachers are the authorities of the hallway, the cheerleaders are the peppy ones. The kids who like science and math are geeks. There's the jocks, the band members, the creative types in art and music. The kids who wear all black are the ones we all avoid and then there is the group of people I belong to:

The popular ones. At Edward Little High we were called The Choice. Why?

Because if asked who would you most want to be friends with, everyone always said us. We were the ultimate choice.

I was the leader, the one everyone wanted to be.

If I wasn't me, I'd want to be me too.

I glanced at the clock on Brett's Audi and snapped my gum. Perfect timing as usual. We would be arriving at the optimum time for everyone to see my entrance. It was the best part of my day. Brett pulled to a stop at the curb and smiled brilliantly from beneath his letterman's jacket.

"Thanks for the ride." I smiled.

"Right here," he said and patted his cheek. I giggled and leaned in to kiss it.

Just before I made contact he turned his head and our lips collided. I kissed him for a minute until his tongue started getting too curious and then pulled back to check my lipstick in the overhead mirror.

"We still on for this weekend?" he asked.

I was getting bored of Brett. "Call me!" I said, and blew him a kiss.

He turned the radio up as I was getting out and "Hurts So Good" played loud behind me.

It was a good song to make an entrance to.

Every girl needs to make an entrance. It's part of her signature.

My hot pink high heels hit the sidewalk and I straightened. My blue jean skirt was brand new and had a bunch of totally rad colorful ruffles on it. My neon green top was spandex and fit like a glove.

On my arm I wore my entire collection of neon bangles. I had them sorted by color so it looked like a rainbow wrapped around my arm. I liked the sound they made when I walked, so I swung my arm just a little more than I needed too.

My blond hair was totally teased. I was having a good bang day. They were super high and I made sure they stayed that way with half a can of hairspray before I left the house. Because I felt like being edgy, I wore a white lace glove on my left hand. By the end of the week everyone would be wearing the same thing.

I started walking down the center of the sidewalk, strutting my stuff like I was a model. The big plastic earrings in my ears moved with every step and I smiled and waved at everyone as I walked by.

"You look fresh, today!" I called to one of the cheerleaders.

"Wasn't that the quarterback of our rival, Allegany High?" my best friend Mandy asked and took up her place beside me.

"He's been driving me all week," I said, wondering why she hadn't noticed until now. She was supposed to pay attention to everything that happened around here. Especially with me, her best friend.

"He's so dreamy," she sighed.

Of course he was. And the leader of The Choice at our rival high school seemed to think so too. I saw her at a party last weekend and she had the nerve to act like my group was somehow less than hers. *I don't think so.* Wonder what she thought now that I was number one in her man's eyes.

I glanced over at Mandy's outfit and rolled my eyes. "Those shoes are grody."

She made a sound. "They look almost exactly like yours, Kelly."

I snapped my gum. "Exactly. You're totally copying."

"It's just shoes."

This was going to require some kind of lesson. She should know better than to try and match my outfits. We'd been friends since third grade, Mandy knew the rules. Her attention to everything going on around her needed some kind of snap back into reality.

"Like, oh my god, did you hear?" Mandy said, totally oblivious to my wrath. "We have a pop quiz in science today."

"Gag me with a spoon," I replied, my eyes sweeping ahead of me as we walked inside the school.

Everyone watched me as Mandy and I made our way to the rest of our group near the lockers. Mandy's boyfriend, Tad, was there as well. He was a jock. If he didn't play soccer, his role wouldn't be so high at school, but he did and he had a nice butt so that made him one of The Choice.

Today he was wearing a pair of white pants that totally hugged his best asset. His short dark hair was styled neat and I smiled.

Once I locked my eyes on a target I always, *always* got what I wanted.

He caught my catlike smile and his cheeks flushed. Beside him was his friend Brandon. I dated him last summer. He was one of my longer relationships, lasting a whole two weeks.

Before me, he'd been dating one of the peppy girls, but one look from me and he forgot her name. Then, he forgot mine.

Refusing to admit defeat, or show even the slightest amount of weakness, I turned the full stare of my baby blues on him. I glanced him up and down, made a sound, and rolled my eyes. "Really, Brandon. Don't you think the phase of wearing mismatched socks is totally past its expiration date? It just isn't cute anymore. In fact, it kind of makes you look a tad bit warped." As I lectured him, I turned toward Mandy and stuck my finger down my throat like I wanted to gag.

Truth was, I used to totally think his mismatched socks were cute. *Not anymore.*

Everyone in our little group laughed. Brandon's face darkened. I saw words form on his lips – some sort of sharp comeback – and I felt the sharp sting of panic.

Maybe I pushed him too far. Maybe asserting my power wasn't a good idea. He could make things hard for me. He could challenge my place at the top with a few nasty words.

I couldn't let that happen.

The panic tasted bitter when I swallowed it down and gave him a totally heinous look. If he took me down, I'd take him down harder. He knew I could do it. I let him see the absolute resolve in my eyes before I dropped them down to stare at the front of his pants.

Brandon blanched. He cleared his throat and averted his gaze.

I spun away, dismissing him completely.

"I'm totally wiggin'," Cindy said. She was wearing a pair of jeans with a flowered tight top. Her earrings were huge plastic circles that touched the side of her neck when she moved. Her dark hair was teased to the max and in the center was a neon headband. "Did you hear about the pop quiz?"

"Totally," I echoed and opened my locker. When I did, I slid a private smile toward Mandy's boyfriend. "Hey, Tad. Would you mind reaching that for me?"

I pointed a perfectly painted nail to the top shelf of my locker at my science book. "I would do it myself, but those geeks back there would totally try and look up my skirt."

He straightened off the lockers and glared at the three geeks across the hall. Two of them actually wore thick framed glasses. One of them had on suspenders. "Beat it, losers!" he yelled.

The geeks took off and I laid my hand on his shoulder. "My hero."

His chest puffed out when he reached for my book.

"What's going on?" Mandy said, coming to stand beside her boyfriend.

"Tad was just being super sweet and getting my book for me. You know how those geeks like to stare." I rolled my eyes and blew a bubble with the pink gum in my mouth.

"So ew." She nodded.

"Mandy, would you totally be a best friend and run to the cafeteria to get me a juice? I forgot to eat this morning and I'm feeling like I'm gonna drop dead."

"Don't you pass the cafeteria on your way to homeroom?" she asked, tucking her books against her chest.

"Don't you want to make it up to me about the shoes?" I pinned her with a direct stare.

She walked off in the direction of the cafeteria and Tad started behind her. I grabbed his arm. "Would you mind staying here? I feel wretched."

Brandon glanced over and gave me a look. I glared daggers at him and he walked away.

"Thank goodness you were here this morning," I told Tad, "Mandy sure is lucky to have you."

"If you ever need anything just yell," he said, tossing back his hair even though it was too short to need tossing. "I'll always be here for Mandy's best friend."

I widened my eyes and stared up at him. "Just because I'm Mandy's best friend?"

He cleared his throat. "Well, no."

"Can you keep a secret, Tad?" I fingered the front of his shirt.

"Of course."

I leaned forward and whispered. "Sometimes I wish I'd met you first."

"Uh… really?" he stuttered.

I nodded and pulled back from him. My heels were so high I teetered a little and made a small shrieking sound.

Before I could fall back into the lockers Tad slipped an arm around my waist and righted me. "Whoa, I think those shoes are dangerous."

I leaned into his chest. "That's the second time today you've saved me."

"It wasn't anything," he said, his eyes dipping down to look at my pink lips.

Inwardly I smiled and leaned even closer, tipping my head back to give him an even better view of my mouth. "How will I ever thank you?"

"No thanks necessary."

"Does Mandy know how lucky she is?" I whispered.

"I'm not sure." He cleared his throat. We were still pressed together and I could feel the rapid beat of his heart.

"Maybe you could give me a ride home from school today?" I asked innocently, dragging a nail down the center of his chest.

"Sure," he bobbed his head up and down.

"Rad." I pulled back and smiled at him.

Seconds later Mandy appeared carrying an orange juice in a plastic container. "Here you go, Kelly. Are you feeling better?"

I glanced at Tad with a secretive expression. "Much. I'll see you in science!" I wagged my fingers at them both and strutted off down the hall.

Everyone I passed by turned to watch me leave. I heard a few whispers, but I didn't need to hear what they were saying. I already knew. The envious looks I got said it all.

The second I turned the corner I tossed the juice in the trash.

By the end of today I'd have Mandy's boyfriend eating out of the palm of my hand.

Chapter TWO

Barf me out – saying this expressed something you do not like.

Eric

D O PEOPLE CHANGE?
Or do they always stay the same?

That's more of a philosophy question. I'm more of a science guy.

I like tangible theories that can be measured, questions with answers that have irrefutable proof. I'm not much for matters of the mind with no exact equation, therefore without exact answer.

I've heard it said that the more people change, the more they stay the same.

That statement is confusing. Whatever "great" mind came up with the saying probably was a philosophy major and had no knowledge of scientific reasoning.

It's a false notion.

A mathematical and scientific fact. In an equation, $a + b = c$. If even just one variable is changed, the entire equation changes, the answer does not remain the same.

If math and science don't give enough irrefutable proof, the world I live in does. In the universe of high school and growing older, everyone changes. It's a natural evolution of life.

I see her every day. Even without my glasses, my eyes would still make out her shape.

She's one of those girls the eyes must look at, just like the lungs must breathe oxygen. Her presence is loud in the hallways of Edward Little High.

Yet her reputation is quiet... at least the real one anyway.

Whispers. I hear them. When you are invisible, or thought to only think about equations and charts, people think you don't listen. But I hear.

I listen.

It's how one learns.

The Choice thinks they know everything, but the people who know the most in this school are the ones who are known the least.

I'm practically a shadow, practically a ghost.

"Beat it, losers!" Tad yells from across the hall. My friends and I look up, surprised he's talking to us.

Okay, maybe I'm not as invisible as I thought.

I glance at Kelly as we scurry off.

Or maybe, I'm only visible when my presence is useful.

I knew Kelly once, a long time ago. Practically in another life. We aren't friends. She probably doesn't even remember my name. I remember hers.

I remember the way she used to twist her Oreos in two and hand me the side with the most cream. The way she would grab my hand and pull me off to play before who we were got in the way.

I remember when she was nice.

As I walk to class, my two friends by my sides, I tune out their conversation and wonder. I saw the way Kelly was looking at Tad, her best friend's boyfriend. It was a sign. Kelly was gearing up to take down another one. It was a pattern. Patterns always repeat themselves.

This time, I wondered if she would go too far.

Kelly was the reason I was spending my time on an internal philosophical debate. Do people change? The theory was no.

I was seeing evidence to the contrary.

The girl I knew all those years ago would never act the way she does now.

But she does.

The whispers follow her around the hall.

People do change.

Sometimes it's not for the better.

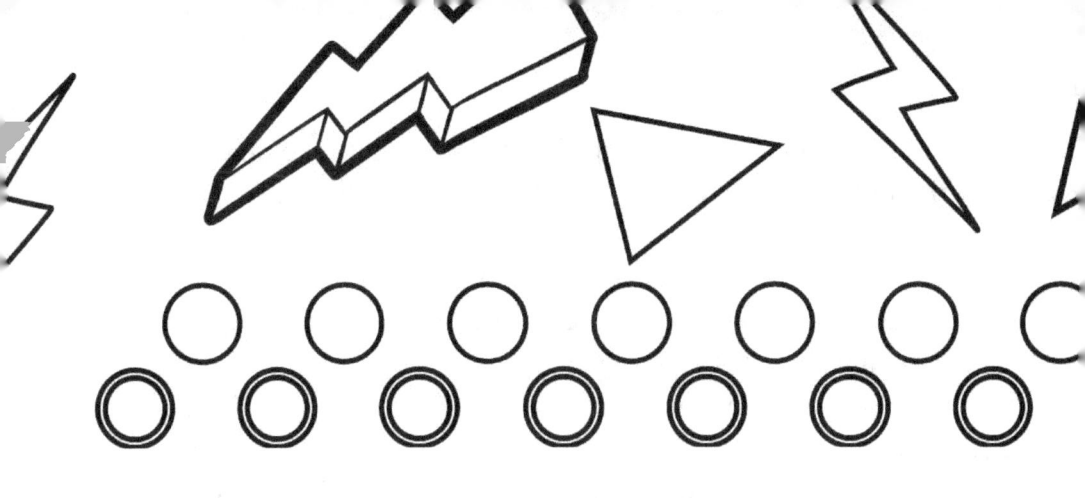

Chapter
THREE

411 – to get information (get the 411)

Kelly

YOU KNOW WHY teachers give pop quizzes? To make our lives just as awful as theirs.

I'm pretty sure I failed the science quiz. It might as well have been in German. Who cared about science anyway? As we exited the class, I glanced out of the corner of my eye at a familiar figure and grimaced.

Science geeks, that's who.

Thank God it was over. I went to my locker, which was already surrounded by my friends, and fixed my lipstick in the small mirror I kept inside. Everyone was already talking about this weekend and the secret party one of the jocks was having at his house because his parents were going to be out of town.

The last party he had pretty much became a legend around here because it was so wild, but somehow the adults never found out. So obviously the anticipation for this one was high.

Mandy leaned up against the locker beside mine, holding her books in front of her and sighed. "I so want to blow off piano lessons and go to the mall. I need a new outfit for the party this weekend."

"Mr. Harvey would totally rat you out to your mom and then you'd never be able to come this weekend," I told her, closing up my lipstick and tossing a few books in my bag.

"I know," she said miserably. "Who cares if I learn to play piano anyway?"

"I thought you liked it?" I pointed out and shut the locker door. Over Mandy's shoulder I saw Tad coming down the hall. I made sure to meet his eyes and smile before looking back at Mandy.

"Well, sure. When it doesn't get in the way of my shopping."

I laughed. "How about we go shopping tomorrow after school? I'm sure getting a ride to the mall will be a piece of cake."

"You could always have Brett drive us," Mandy said, smiling ruefully. "His Audi is totally hot."

I smiled and leaned in and whispered. "So is he."

Tad stepped into earshot right behind Mandy. "He is definitely easy to look at."

Tad frowned. "Mandy!" I said, pretending to be shocked. "You have a boyfriend."

"I can look," she shrugged.

I cleared my throat loudly and straightened making sure to smile widely. "Oh, hey, Tad!"

Mandy's eyes widened and then she spun around. "Hey, babe."

"Who are you talking about?" he asked, searching her eyes. "Who?"

"The guy you are just looking at?" he replied, smoothly.

Mandy waved his comment off. "No one. Just the guy Kelly is going with."

Tad glanced up. "You're going with someone?"

"I'm not going with him. He just wants me to." I replied, and tossed my hair over my shoulder.

"Even better, he'll totally drive us to the mall if he's trying to get you to date him," Mandy said.

"When?" Tad asked.

"Tomorrow," Mandy answered. "I need clothes."

He rolled his eyes. "You have enough clothes for half the school."

"I wish!" she said. Mandy bounced up and kissed him on the cheek. "Gotta get to Mr. Harvey's room or I'll be late."

"See ya," he said.

"Call me!" she said, but I wasn't sure if she meant me or Tad.

When she was gone I smiled at him.

"Still need that ride home?" he asked.

"For sure."

"C'mon," he gestured and we walked down the hall together toward the exit doors leading to the parking lot.

Tad drove a red Ford Capri and it was always spotless. That told me how much he loved his car.

"I love your car," I sighed, like it was dreamy. "It's so rad you have your own."

"Makes it easy to get around," he said and opened the passenger door for me. I moved to get by, my body coming into contact with his. His eyes flared, but he didn't say anything.

He didn't have to, I knew he liked it.

In a way, I was doing Mandy a favor. Clearly Tad was a cheater waiting to happen.

I watched him jog around to the driver's side and slide in. When he looked over at me, I gave him a smile.

"What kind of music do you listen to?" he asked, opening up the glove box to reveal a ton of cassette tapes.

"I like just about everything," I said.

He plucked one up and slid it into the tape deck. Music filled the car as he fired up the engine.

"You going to Aaron's party this weekend?" I asked. "It's probably going to be tubular."

"Wouldn't miss it!" He nodded.

"Think Mandy would mind if I borrowed you for a dance?" I reached over and ran a finger down his arm.

His cheeks flushed and he shook his head.

Some guys were just too easy.

For most of the ride home I asked him about himself, the sports he played, his car. He ate it up and I choked it down.

He was a nice enough guy, I guess. But man, he was just too eager. I wondered if he agreed with everything I said because he was agreeable, or if he just thought that's what I wanted to hear.

Thankfully, it wasn't a long ride to my house and soon we were pulling in the driveway. "Did you want to come in for a minute?" I asked. "My mom makes great cookies."

Please say no.

"Wish I could, but I have practice."

"Now?" I gasped.

He nodded.

"I hope I didn't make you late?"

"Nah, it's cool. Coach won't care. Besides, couldn't just leave you to walk. A beautiful girl like you just might disappear."

I giggled. "You think I'm beautiful?"

"Everyone does."

"Do you think I'm prettier than Mandy?" I asked. "Because I think she's gorgeous."

He hesitated.

I leaned forward and rested my hand on his arm. "Forget it. That was a terrible question to ask. Of course you think she's prettier than me."

His hand covered mine. "Actually, I think you're prettier. But don't tell her I said that."

"My lips are sealed." I smiled. "Well! I better run. I've made you late enough!"

"I'll get the door for you." He hurried out of the car and around to open up the passenger side for me.

"Thank you," I said. "You're a gentleman. Too bad you were already taken. Thanks for the ride." I gave him a little wave and started away.

"So if I wasn't," he paused, "taken, would you be interested?"

I smiled a catlike smile before I turned back.

"Of course. Who wouldn't be?" I said. My eyes widened and I rushed over toward him. "Please don't tell Mandy I said that. I feel just awful! She's my best friend. It's just…"

"Just…" he prodded.

"Just sometimes it upsets me when she looks at other guys. You know how she said she thought Brett was hot? He's not the first guy she's said that about. You're just such a great guy. I mean look, you're making yourself late to a practice just so I didn't have to walk home."

"She checks out a lot of guys?" he asked, frowning.

"She just looks." I waved it away. "As far as I know. It's really not a big deal."

"Right," he said, totally unconvinced.

"I upset you." I frowned.

"Guys don't like to hear their girlfriends are looking around at other guys," he explained.

I went forward and hugged him. "I'm sorry."

I smiled into his shirt when he hugged me back. I lingered a few seconds before pulling away. "I just thought you needed to know."

He nodded. "Thanks for telling me."

He started to walk away, but I grasped his hand. "Tad?"

"Yeah?"

I went forward and pressed my lips to his. I felt his shock, but it instantly changed and he kissed me back. I didn't let it go on for long, and there definitely wasn't any tongue.

When I pulled back, I swiped at his lower lip where there was some lipstick and smiled. "For luck today at practice."

"Thanks," he mumbled, looking a little dazed. When he walked back to his car, I couldn't help but notice a little extra swagger in his step.

I stood there and watched him pull away. He waved through the window and I waved back.

Soon as he was out of sight, I walked to my front door. Tad was just like the rest of these guys. Predictable.

He'd be mine by the end of the week.

Chapter FOUR

Bag your face! – a colorful way to tell someone
to shut up.

Eric

MY BAGS WERE PACKED and sitting beside the front door when I got home from science club. I might have been alarmed if it wasn't for the chaos going on beyond the bags.

Well, that and the fact my bags weren't the only ones by the door. Clearly, this wasn't me being tossed out of my own house for no apparent reason.

In the background there was some annoying sound accompanied by new voices. "Mom!" I yelled over them.

"Eric," Mom said, appearing from the direction of the family room. "I didn't realize it was already this late."

"Uh, what's going on?" I asked. "Shouldn't you still be at work?"

My mom worked for a local doctor's office as a receptionist. She worked good hours, but it was still early for her to be home.

"I should be, but the family room has become our own personal indoor pool," she replied with a sigh.

Obviously, this was something I had to see for myself. I dropped my book bag by the rest of my packed stuff and headed toward our new pool.

The second I stepped down into the sunken living room, my shoes made a squishing sound. I would have looked down, but I was too busy staring at the water dripping from a hole in the ceiling.

The plaster was soaked and crumbling, and part of the section still where it *should* be looked heavy and bowed. The water stain, while clearly the least of our worries, was still epically large and commanded some attention.

There were two men in white jumpsuits with these big vacuums (that would be the loud sound and strange voices I heard) sucking up the puddles of water that saturated everything.

I stepped further into the room, my shoes sucking up the water like a sponge, and looked up into the hole where the ceiling use to be.

I was no plumber, but I knew a burst pipe when I saw one. This one hadn't just burst either, it exploded. The metal pipe hung crookedly from the ceiling, a huge hole in its side—so large the pipe was almost in half. Water dripped from it every so often and landed on the men below.

"How did this happen?" I asked.

"Bad pipe," one of the men shouted over the vacuum.

Really? I wouldn't have guessed.

I backtracked out of the family room to where my mom hovered in the door. "I don't know," she said. "I got a call from Gladys next door. I guess she heard the sound of the ceiling coming down when she was gardening outside and called me at work."

"For once, her nosiness comes in handy," I quipped, pushing at the glasses on my nose.

Mom smothered a smile. "Now, Eric, be polite."

That *was* polite. I didn't bother to point it out though. Clearly Mom had a bad enough day. Course, most moms would probably be shrieking and having a fit about their carpet and furniture right about now. She wasn't though, she just seemed mildly annoyed.

But my mom's dealt with worse. Something like a burst pipe probably seems like a piece of cake compared to what my father put her through.

"So, I'm guessing the bags by the door mean this mess won't be cleaned up by tonight?" I asked.

"I'm afraid not. And due to the hole in the pipe, the water for the entire house is shut off until it can be replaced. Since this happened they're also going to check around to make sure we don't have any other pipes about to blow."

"How long until it's fixed?" I was already making a list of things I wanted to grab from my room.

"Probably a week or so. Hopefully cleaning the water up now will minimize the damage to the room and it can dry out. Then the ceiling will need to be repaired."

"We can't just stay here?" I asked. Staying in a hotel room with my mom was the very last thing on my list of life goals. In fact, it was the last thing *after* my last thing. I'd rather hang out with Pee-Wee Herman than sleep in a bed right beside her every night for the foreseeable future.

"We need water, Eric, and the men need to be able to work without worrying about disturbing us."

"How are we going to pay for all this?"

For the first time since I walked in the house, a stressed look came into her eyes. I felt bad for saying that before I thought it through. I was pretty positive we didn't have the money for this. By the looks of things, it wasn't going to be a cheap repair. Plus a week in a hotel... that was going to cost.

"Don't you worry about that," she replied, quickly getting rid of the stress on her face. "I've got it taken care of."

I wasn't going to tell her I knew she was lying. Anger at my father filled me. I knew the burst pipe wasn't his fault, but everything else was. The reason she was lying to me was.

"I'm just gonna go grab a few things out of my room," was all I said, and headed toward the stairs.

She nodded. "I already packed your clothes and things."

"Thanks," I said. "Give me a minute then we can go to the hotel."

I was halfway up the stairs when she said, "We aren't staying at a hotel."

"Where are we staying then?" I asked.

"Marcie Ross has invited us to stay at her home."

"We're staying at the Ross's?" I asked. Maybe I inhaled too many chemicals in science club today. I could have sworn she just said I would be staying at Kelly Ross's house.

"Well, yes. Wasn't it nice of Marcie to ask? It will be much more comfortable for us than a hotel."

Comfortable was not the word that described what I was feeling right now. I must have had a constipated look on my face because Mom frowned.

"I thought you and Kelly were friends? You used to play all the time."

"That was in first grade, Mom."

"So you aren't friends anymore?" she asked, shifting a little, like it was just occurring to her that maybe this arrangement would be less than ideal.

Kelly doesn't even know my name.

"We, uh, sort of belong in different circles," I said. Why I felt the need to sort of defend the fact Kelly would rather die than talk to me or acknowledge we used to know each other at all was something I didn't want to think about.

"Well, this will give you a chance to reconnect," she said with a broad smile.

Parents were delusional. It's like the minute they graduate, they get a bad case of amnesia and forget how brutal high school really is.

Once again, I said nothing. At least this way Mom wouldn't have to pay for a hotel. That definitely would help with expenses.

I continued up the stairs to my room. I was going to be living with Kelly Ross for a week.

The most popular girl at school.

The most un-liked girl at Edward Little High. I wonder if Kelly knew I would soon be invading her perfect little world?

She was not going to be happy.

Not like I was jumping for joy either. At least her house was big. Maybe I could avoid her all week. I could pretend I was at the hotel that just minutes ago I had been wishing I didn't have to stay in.

Be careful what you wish for, you just might get it.

Me, Eric the science geek, in the same house as Kelly the maneater?

This was going to be interesting.

Chapter FIVE

Burn Out – a druggie. Usually a derogatory term.

Kelly

W HEN YOU'RE SMALL, life is uncomplicated. It doesn't matter who you are so much because you have the freedom to figure it out. You don't have to think about other people's opinions, or how the people you chose to surround yourself is a direct reflection of yourself.

Life was simpler back then. I still remember running around with my hair in tangles, bare feet and chocolate on my mouth. I was carefree. My biggest worry was what time I had to go to bed and being inside before it got out dark out.

My best friend in the world was a boy and we didn't like-like each other—there was no competition between us, there was no pressure at all. We just were friends.

Time passes though, and relationships change. People pull away and others yank you in a different direction.

One day you look at the person you thought you would always know… and they're a stranger.

"I can't believe you invited them to stay here!" I told my mother. "How embarrassing!"

My mother looked up from the dinner she was making. "How is offering a friend a place to stay when their home is under construction embarrassing?"

"He's not in the same crowd as me, mother," I said, barely holding on to my patience. She would never understand.

"I didn't know you had to be in the same crowd with someone to be nice to them," she observed, almost like this conversation was boring to her.

"What will people say?" I worried. "A science geek in my house!"

Mom set down the big spoon she was using to put the meatloaf into a pan and looked at me as I paced.

By the way, I was looking totally fresh in a pair of hot pink leggings, purple leg warmers and a white top that totally showed off one of my shoulders. My hair was still teased to perfection. When I got home I gave it a backcomb and then sprayed it with some extra White Rain just to make sure it stayed.

"I thought you and Eric were friends."

"That was a whole other lifetime ago!"

"Kelly Ann Ross, I expect you to be nice to that boy. His mother is a dear friend of mine and I will not have you being anything but the girl I raised you to be toward her son."

"Yes, ma'am," I muttered.

"Especially after everything he's been through," Mom went back to her meatloaf.

"What do you mean?" I asked picking up a carrot stick and biting into it.

"It doesn't matter. Being nice matters."

"You sound like an after school special." I rolled my eyes.

"Kelly!" my mom admonished. "I'm serious."

What would Mandy say when she found out? What would Tad think? And Brett? My reputation was on the line here.

"Remember that time you got your hair stuck in the chain on the swing in the backyard and you cried and cried and cried?" Mom mused, like it was a fond memory.

"Of course I remember," I replied, eating another carrot. "I was sure my hair was going to rip out at the root. The way it pinched and tugged, it hurt so bad!"

Mom nodded. "I could hear you screaming from all the way upstairs in my bedroom. By the time I got downstairs though, Eric was already getting you free."

I smiled a little at the memory. I guess it had been kind of funny.

We'd been on the swing, twisting it around and around as we took turns sitting on it. When we let, go the swing spun around wildly as it unwound and the entire world rushed by in a blur, leaving me feeling slightly woozy.

It had been fun, up until my long blond hair got twisted up with the chain and almost ripped it out. That first tug hurt like the devil and I remember digging my heels into the ground to stop the swing from turning anymore.

I tried to get free, but my hair was so knotted the more I tried the worse it got. I cried and screamed, panic and pain had taken over my mind so much I could barely think.

At first Eric thought I was kidding. I always did like to play jokes... *What ever happened to that side of me?* But he quickly realized I wasn't joking when the tears started falling over my cheeks and I fought with the chain and my hair.

He ran away.

His eyes got big as saucers and off he went.

I cried even harder when I realized he wasn't going to help me.

But, seconds later, the back door of the house slammed and he reappeared. In his arms was a tub of margarine from the refrigerator.

He looked blurry through my tear stained eyes as he approached.

"It's okay, Kelly," he said. "I'll help you. That's what friends do, they help each other."

I stopped crying then, even when my scalp hurt every time the swing moved. Eric used the entire tub of margarine and buttered up my hair and the chain. It felt like it took forever, but it worked, he slipped my hair right out of the chain and I was able to dash free.

Mom laughed at the sight of me, all covered in butter. I couldn't be the only one looking so ridiculous, so I tackle hugged Eric and smeared butter all over him.

Before we could go inside, Mom made us hose ourselves off.

We spent half the afternoon that day playing in the garden hose without a care to how we looked.

"You two were inseparable."

"Until he stopped coming around," I mumbled.

"What?" she looked up.

"Nothing," I replied and turned to escape to my room.

The doorbell rang through the house and I quickened my steps.

"Kelly! Can you get that, my hands are a mess!"

Damn! I wasn't quick enough. Instead of running to my room to hide, I went and pulled open the front door.

Eric's mom stood on the front porch. She looked like she always had, with dark, permed hair and brown eyes. She was wearing scrubs, she'd probably just come from work, and in her hand was a small suitcase.

"Hi, Mrs. Seaver," I said, opening the door wider. "Please come in."

"Hi, Kelly honey. Don't you just look so grown up? It's been ages since I've seen you."

I couldn't remember the last time I saw her. Usually when she and my mom got together I was at school or something.

"And you know you can call me Laurie. Especially now since we are going to be roommates for a week."

An entire week? Kill me now!

I knew Eric was hovering outside on the porch, but he hadn't stepped forward when his mom had come in so I started to close the door.

I didn't get it very far when I felt resistance on the other side. Sighing, I looked around the dark wood to see Eric there, with a bored look on his face, a bag in his hand and the other splayed on the front door as he pushed it open.

"Oh, I didn't see you there," I lied.

"Well come on, Eric. We're not trying to invite in the bugs," his mother admonished.

He walked right in without looking at me.

How rude.

"Do you two see each other often at school?" his mom asked.

I smiled. "Not often."

"We have a class together," he said.

"Oh, well maybe you help each other with homework while we're here."

We were saved from answering to that when my mom breezed into the room. "Laurie! So glad you made it. So how bad is the mess at your house?"

The two started talking about water mess, burst pipes, and stuff I had no desire to listen to.

That left me with him.

I glanced up. He was looking at me.

"Hey, Kelly," Eric said.

"Hi," I echoed.

"I'll show you to your rooms," Mom said, waving at them to follow along. "I'm so glad you could come and stay. Dinner will be ready in just a while. I have a meatloaf in the oven."

"Meatloaf!" Laurie exclaimed. "That's Eric's favorite!"

"I remember," my mom said.

I suppressed the urge to roll my eyes.

I started forward, ready to leave him in my dust.

"Kelly," Mom called behind her. "Why don't you show Eric his room? It's the guest room right across the hall from your room."

Gag me with a spoon. I wanted to die.

I glanced over my shoulder at him. "Come on."

He followed without a word. Upstairs in the hall, I pointed out his room. Before he could go in, I gave him a hard stare. "Do not tell anyone about this at school."

"What's the matter?" he asked. "Afraid your precious reputation will go to hell?"

My mouth dropped open.

He smirked. "Don't worry, Kelly. I won't say a word. I don't want anyone to know I'm here either."

"You don't?" I echoed, surprised. I thought he'd be shouting it down the halls. I mean, *him* staying with Kelly Ross?

He'd be instantly popular, and I'd be a laughingstock.

"No," he said, his voice flat.

I felt my mouth drop open again.

Eric let himself in his "new room" and before I could recover, shut the door in my face.

Chapter SIX

Deep shit – a way to say you are in trouble.

Eric

I DON'T KNOW WHY she acted so surprised. Did she really think I'd be jumping up and down at being here? I know she was used to people at school tripping over themselves to even get her to smile at them, but I'm not one of those people.

To me, Kelly was human just like everyone else. Even more so because I knew who she used to be a long time ago.

Maybe it was unfair to judge her based on how she was as a child. But isn't that when people are the most pure? Isn't that when they are most who they are before all the other stuff (like life) got in the way?

If I was truthful, that applied to me. I was more jaded now than when I was a kid, I just showed it in a different way.

'Course, I had a reason to be jaded. Kelly didn't.

Three days of living at her house with her family. It really wasn't that hard to avoid her. I got up and went to school before her, and spent the extra time in the science lab. I just grabbed something quick for breakfast and ate it at the school. Kelly got up later and arrived at her usual time.

It was like it had always been during the day.

Like I didn't exist. Hell, she even told my mom we never saw each other. Was I really that invisible? Did she really not know I was in her science class?

I'd spend some extra time after school in the library, at science club or with a friend. By the time I got home at night it was almost dinner. That was when it got a little awkward.

We all ate together, like a happy family.

Me, my mom, Kelly, her mom and her dad. Except for the night her dad was working late.

Thankfully we didn't have to talk much because our mothers never shut up.

After dinner I'd go up to my room and do homework or listen to music. Sometimes as I laid there with my Walkman and headphones, I'd stare at the closed door and know she was just across the hall. What was she doing?

A couple times I heard her laugh. She was probably on the phone. Probably talking to her latest victim. I was pretty sure that victim was Mandy's boyfriend.

More proof that people change. The girl I use to know would never betray a friend.

Isn't that what she did to you?

That really wasn't fair, I guess. She wasn't the only one to blame for the reason we stopped being friends.

"Earth to Mr. Seaver," Mr. Brawn sang.

I snapped out of my thoughts and sat up, nearly knocking my book off the desk. I caught it just in time.

People laughed.

"What?" I asked, righting the book.

"Are you paying attention?" he asked, a puzzled look on his face. I'd never not paid attention before.

"Of course, I just didn't hear you."

He repeated the question and I rattled off the answer. He seemed satisfied and went back to the front of the room. Good thing I read ahead last night.

Actually, I'd done all the reading for the entire week.

Clearly, living in that house was getting to me. I couldn't even pay attention in my favorite class.

"I have the pop quiz scores here," Mr. Brawn said, holding up a stack of papers. Everyone groaned.

"I have to say, some of you totally bombed. Maybe if you spent as much time on your classwork as you do your hair, these grades would look better."

He started handing out the worksheets with the grades and everyone shifted around nervously.

"If you totally failed," the teacher went on as he passed them out, "you can do an extra credit assignment. A two page report on the topic of your choice. Obviously in some relation to science."

He handed me my paper and I took it. There was an A in red marker on the top. I really hadn't expected anything less.

The guy next to me wasn't so lucky. He had a D + on his paper.

What a moron. It wasn't even a hard quiz.

I heard a familiar voice, rather, a familiar groan, and glanced two seats up and one row over. Kelly was staring at her paper. I knew from her body language she wasn't too happy but I couldn't see the mark.

As I watched her, she leaned back to whisper to someone behind her and I saw the letter grade marking the top of her quiz.

Yikes.

She did worse than the moron beside me.

When she pulled back from the girl she was whispering to, our eyes met. She made a face and spun around in her seat.

The bell rang and everyone rushed from the room.

My friend Ryan was waiting in the hall. He was in the science club too. He always wore suspenders, which I thought were dorky, but I'd never tell him that.

"We still on for this weekend?" he asked.

We'd been planning to get together at my place and watch the VHS of The Amityville Horror. My mom always went to bed early, so we knew we could get away with watching it without being caught.

Ryan was a total horror movie junkie. I guess I kind of was too. It's not like there was much else to do around here. Neither one of us had a car, and even if we did, the options were limited to the mall and the arcade.

Ryan's mom hated scary movies and never let him watch them (which in my opinion only made him want to watch them more) so we watched them at my house.

"Can do it at your place?" I asked.

"You know my mom will flip," Ryan said. "What's wrong with your place?"

"Ah, plumbing problems," I said. I hadn't even told him where I was staying right now. "Burst pipe, the family room is out of commission."

"Sucks," Ryan said. "Sure, come to my place. Maybe my mom will go to bed early."

"Will do." A couple jocks ran down the center of the hallway and knocked into Ryan and all his books went flying.

"Jerks!" I yelled after them.

"Whoa!" Ryan said and pressed against my shoulder like he thought I was going to rush them and start a fight.

They hadn't even heard me. They were already down the hall and turning the corner. They didn't notice, or didn't care, who they plowed in to.

"What the heck was that?" he asked, bending down to get his stuff.

I helped, picking up a nearby folder and pen.

"Nothing. I'm just tired of the way some people act in this school. Always acting like they are better than everyone else."

"It's been that way for years, why you so mad about it now?"

"Maybe I've always been mad about it," I snapped.

Ryan fell silent as we started walking again.

"Look. I'm sorry. They just make me mad is all."

He nodded. "I get it. So I'll see you at my place this weekend?"

"Absolutely," I agreed.

I didn't bother hanging around school extra today, I was tired of being around the people. I felt edgy kind of, distracted. Just like I was in science today.

Soon as I got to the Ross's house I went straight to the phone hanging on the wall and dialed the doctor's office my mom worked at.

"Dr. Brawn's practice. How can I help you today?" Mom was cheerful.

"Hey, Mom. It's me."

"Eric, hi!" She paused. "Is something wrong?"

I never called her at work, so of course she would think that. Technically, there was something wrong. I wanted the hell out of this house.

"No, I'm fine. I'm just here at the Ross's…"

"Yeah?" she asked. I could hear the steady murmur of voices in the background from the waiting room.

"How is the house coming along? We moving back in soon?"

She sighed. "I'm afraid not. The plumber just called. It's going to be several more days. He found some other pipes that needed replacing."

"Oh come on!" I griped.

"Eric," Mom said, surprise in her voice.

"Sorry," I hurried to say. "I uh, well I was supposed to have Ryan over this weekend."

"I'm sorry, honey. Set it up for next weekend. I'll get you guys a pizza."

I leaned my forehead against the wall as I held the receiver to my ear. "Sounds great."

"Great," she said.

"Hey, Mom," I said before she could hang up.

"Yes?"

"Did he tell you how much it's gonna be?"

The long pause on the other end was answer enough.

Finally she answered, her voice hesitant. "He gave me an estimate, yes."

"We can't afford it can we?" I said into the line.

"Well it's more than I was hoping," she said, trying to make it sound better than it was. "The plumber said I could make payments. I was going to call down to the diner Grandpa use to own and see if I could pick up some waitressing shifts on the weekends for a few weeks and make some extra money."

"I'll get a job," I said.

"Absolutely not," she insisted.

"I'm almost eighteen, Mom. Most kids my age already work."

"You're priority is school. That's it. You have the rest of your life to work."

We'd had this conversation before, and it was always the same. I wanted to get a job and help out and she always said no.

One of these days I was just going to get a job anyway. It's not like she could stop me.

"I have to go, okay? A patient is waiting."

"Okay."

"I'll see you in just a bit."

I hung up and looked around the empty kitchen for a few minutes. The Ross's always did have money. Kelly's dad had a really good job and provided for his family.

Some fathers did that.

Anger, just like I felt at school in the hall, shot through me. I picked up the phone again and punched in a number I knew but barely ever called.

"Mr. Seaver's office," a woman said into the line.

"This is Eric Seaver. I'd like to speak with him please."

"Hold, please."

Some lousy elevator music came on the line and I stood there waiting. Then I waited some more. I was just about to hang up when his voice came on the line.

"Eric?"

"Yeah, dad," I said.

"I'm surprised to hear from you," my father said into the line. He talked kind of in a brusque tone. He was a busy man; he owned a car dealership. The most successful one in town. Most people were impressed by that, but I wasn't. I wasn't impressed by anything about him.

"I'm calling for a reason," I said, getting right to it. "We've had some stuff happen at the house. Burst pipes and stuff."

"Yeah?"

"Mom can't afford to fix it. She's talking about getting a second job."

"I see," he said, sounding less hurried. He knew what I wanted. "You know I'm remarried now, son."

"I never ask you for anything. I'm asking you for this," I said, my hand fisting at my side.

I never wanted to be like him. Never. I never talked to him. I wouldn't have called today, but I couldn't let my mom get a second job. She did enough already. If talking to him would help her, then I would do it.

"How much?" he asked, his voice low.

"Five hundred," I said. I had no idea how much the pipes were going to cost but five hundred was a lot and it should be enough.

He made a sound.

"You owe this to us," I said into the phone, my voice not backing down.

"Fine. I'll have my secretary cut a check and send it to the house."

"We aren't there," I said, not showing any of my shock or relief that he actually agreed. "Send it to the office where she works."

"Fine," he agreed.

He didn't even ask where we were. If I was okay.

"Thanks," I forced the word through my lips and then slammed the phone down.

I pressed both hands on the wall on either side of the phone and took a deep breath. Mom was going to be pissed I called him, but I didn't care. I was right. He owed us.

You think I'd be used to this feeling by now.

"Who was that?" a familiar voice butted in from behind.

I spun away from the wall to find Kelly. She was standing in the kitchen staring at me. Her blond hair was poufy around her face, her lips were pink and she was dressed in a pair of Jordache jeans and a tight, bright pink top that showed off her flat stomach.

"No one," I said.

"It obviously wasn't no one."

"You're right," I conceded. "It wasn't no one. It was someone. But it still isn't your business."

"You can't talk to me like that."

"Why? Because you're the most popular girl at school?" I rolled my eyes. "Newsflash, I couldn't care less."

She made a sound kind of like a huff and stomped forward. Her glare was icy. In fact, if I'd touched, her I might have gotten frostbite.

But I didn't move.

I planted my feet into the floor. If she thought she could glare at me with those blue eyes and I'd be intimidated like everyone else and back down, she was wrong.

"Move," she demanded when she realized I wasn't going anywhere.

"Make me," I said calmly.

I might be a "geek" but I wasn't a wimp. I was taller than her. Not by some great length, but still taller. I wasn't bulky like the jocks and I wasn't ripped with muscles, but still, I was broader, and if I didn't want to move she wouldn't be able to change that.

"Whatever," she muttered, stepping around me, and fled the room.

I probably should have felt good I finally got the better of someone who claimed to be the best.

Too bad it only made me feel worse.

Chapter SEVEN

Wastoid – a waste of space. An insult.

Kelly

I WAS STILL FUMING.

Absolutely furious!

How dare Eric talk to me like that? And in my own kitchen!

I ought to rat him out to his mother and watch him try to worm his way out of that one. I smirked at the thought. It would be fun to see.

I could tell he was a momma's boy. So totally lame.

But the way he'd stood up to me earlier, refusing to move... Not something I expected.

No one ever challenged me. Ever. If they did? I made sure they never did it again.

Eric had to know this. There was no trace of wariness or even regret in his eyes when he stared at me. It was like he wasn't scared of me at all.

I kinda like it. I shoved the thought away, but it still persisted. I couldn't help but respect and even be intrigued by the fact Eric wasn't intimidated by me.

I was used to everyone scurrying to do my bidding.

Clearly, he wasn't going to.

Like I said, I could challenge him. Totally make his life hell and go to his mother. I wasn't going to do that though.

Aside from the fact that I'd gained some respect for him today, I saw how he was acting when I walked into the kitchen. He'd been having a conversation on the phone with someone he clearly didn't like. The way he slammed the receiver down… well, I kinda forgot he was a geek.

For a moment anyway.

He'd been angry. When he spun around, I saw a moment of pain in his eyes before he hid it away.

It made me curious.

Most people were open books, which was a good thing considering I didn't really read much.

Not Eric, though. Eric's cover was closed, his pages were pressed together tight.

He was a book I wanted to read. The mystery between his pages called to me like a really good sale at the mall.

I wanted to open him up, find the page where I'd last left off and read and read until I'd devoured all the words.

During dinner I found myself sneaking glances at him out of the corner of my eye. He looked like he did the day before… but somehow different.

Eric had dark hair, so dark it was almost black. It was kind of curly, and fell over his forehead and made him look like a puppy dog.

Excerpt for tonight. Tonight the way the curls fell it was like they were rebelling, like they did whatever they wanted to do and what they wanted was to touch his skin.

His eyes were brown, a light brown that contrasted with the dark shock of all his hair. I never really noticed before how they seemed to light up his entire face, even from behind the black framed glasses he wore.

He hadn't gotten glasses until second grade. People at school made fun of him when he first showed up with them on his face. I never said anything, I never defended him.

At the time, I secretly thought he deserved it.

That thought made me lose my appetite and the dinner on my plate no longer looked appealing.

I never noticed how tall he was until earlier either, when I'd stood almost toe to toe with him and challenged him to move. When we were little, I was taller than him. My mom always said girls grow faster than boys, but I had never thought about that much until today.

He'd caught up.

I had to tilt my gaze up to meet his now.

When I tried to look past his shoulders, I couldn't. They were too broad for my eyes to stare off into space behind him. It was like everything about Eric commanded my attention today.

It was totally annoying.

Just like this stupid grade. I was a total airhead. I knew Mr. Brawn was for sure talking about me when he said people cared too much about their hair. Like caring about your appearance was a crime or something.

I wouldn't care except this was totally going to bring down my average. If I brought home a bunch of lame grades I'd be in deep shit.

And I could kiss a car goodbye for my eighteenth birthday.

Extra credit it was. I had to write a two page paper on something scientific. Kill me now. The least the teacher could have done was give us a topic. How was I supposed to know what to write about?

I stared down at the blank notebook page in front of me and sighed. I needed to at least get a start on this. The party was this weekend and I wouldn't have time to sit around and worry about it the entire time. If I at least had a topic, and maybe some of it started, I would be in much better shape.

Giving up on trying to pick a topic on my own, I reached for my science textbook to thumb through it and hopefully find something I could study and write about that wouldn't bore me to tears or require me to turn my kitchen into a makeshift science lab.

As I shuffled through the pages, Eric walked in. The second he saw me at the table he stopped. "I didn't know you were in here," he said.

When he first walked in the house, I thought for sure he'd be "bumping" into me all the time, maybe even trying to get rides with me to school. None of those things happened. If anything, he seemed even more determined to avoid me than I was him.

"There's soda in the fridge," I said.

He nodded and went over to get himself a Coke. It made a popping sound when he popped the top. I looked up as he tilted the can to this mouth and became entranced by the way his throat moved as he swallowed the carbonated beverage.

He was wearing a plain white t-shirt over his jeans. One of the sleeves was rolled up higher than the other, and it made him look totally dorky. But it also exposed more of his bicep.

"What?" he asked, pulling the can down and staring at me pointedly.

"Nothing," I muttered and looked back down at my book.

I couldn't even tell you what I was looking at though. His presence was a complete distraction. Even though I refused to look at him again, I felt him standing there. He was watching me—the attention made the back of neck feel hot.

What the hell was wrong with me?

People looked at me all the time. It wasn't anything new.

My skin never prickled when they did, though. I never once felt like I was under a microscope and everything about me was being studied up close.

It was a test I wasn't sure I'd pass, just like that dumb pop quiz.

The sound of him moving closer made my toes jump against the floor beneath the table. I gripped my pencil a little tighter as he moved by.

Eric stopped, picked up the corner of my science book and tilted it toward him. "Extra credit?" he asked.

I nodded, still staring down. His fingers were long, and kind of thick. His thumbnail was slightly jagged, like he might bite it when he was studying or something.

I fought the urge to look up.

"I totally spaced on that quiz. I have to bring the grade up."

He let go of my book and his fingers left my line of sight. "Have fun with that."

"Hey," I said as he was leaving.

He stopped and turned. His dark eyebrow lifted, arching over the top of his glasses.

I never really noticed how good he looked in them before.

"Um, you're good at science. What should I write the paper on?"

"You're asking me?" he said, a smirk on his face.

"Well isn't science like your mothership or something?" I muttered. "You're Mr. Brawn's favorite."

"Oh, so you do know we're in the same class," he scoffed and drank some more of the soda.

"Never mind," I snapped. He was impossible! He never used to be such a pain in the ass.

I went back to the book, forcing all my attention away from him.

I expected him to leave, to go back to the room he was staying in and for me not to see him again until tomorrow night at dinner.

He didn't leave.

The legs of the wooden chair beside mine made a scraping sound when he dragged it out and sat down. His soda can hit the table near my book and then he slid it out from under me and in front of him.

"What are you doing?"

"You asked me for help." Why did he sound so amused by this? He probably thought I was stupid because I got a bad grade.

I admit, school wasn't necessarily my top priority, but I wasn't a bad student. I just wasn't in the running for valedictorian like he was.

He started flipping through my book.

"Hey," I said and reached for it. "I didn't ask you to sit down and become commander of my book."

He snatched it out of my grasp and grinned. He had very straight teeth. And his lips were like this dark shade of pink.

"Do you want my help or not?" he asked.

I made a face and he laughed.

He knew I needed his help and he was enjoying it.

I gave him a death glare and he acted like he didn't even notice. Seconds later he slid the book back in front of me. It was open to a page toward the back of the book, where we hadn't been to yet in class.

"Do it on this." He tapped his finger on the page.

I leaned forward and looked down. "Astronomy?" I asked.

"Stars," he said. "You know those things that light up in the sky?"

"I know what astronomy is, butthead."

"Well after that grade you got today I wasn't so sure."

"You totally looked at my paper!" I accused. I felt my cheeks turning hot and I knew I was blushing. I was embarrassed about the grade, but more than anything I was embarrassed he saw it.

He'd probably never gotten that low of a grade ever.

"You were the one holding it up for everyone to see."

"Was not!"

Eric smirked and lifted the soda to sit back in the chair and take a drink.

I glanced back down at the book. "So you think I should write a report about the stars?"

"The constellations." He nodded. "We don't have much time at the end of the year for this unit, so there's lots of stuff that he won't cover. He'll like that you are learning something he doesn't have time to teach."

"I don't know anything about the stars." I flipped through the pages. "Guess I'll have to read all this."

He laughed. "You sound like somebody died."

"Reading is boring."

"Maybe you just haven't found something you like to read."

"Maybe," I echoed. "But I know it's not this book."

He was easy to talk to. He always had been. Even when we were little, I remember how much I liked just being in his presence and how we would talk about everything.

Course, when we were in first grade everything consisted of cartoons and made up games.

"I have a better idea," he said.

I glanced up.

"C'mon." He stood up and pushed in his chair. "Let's go."

"Go where?" I asked, surprised.

"You'll see."

"You could just tell me," I said.

"You're used to always getting your way aren't you?"

"Nothing wrong with that," I defended.

"No. But doesn't that get boring?"

"Of course not," I scoffed.

But, with him towering over my chair, a little mystery in his eyes and that question coming off his lips....

Maybe it was a little boring.

When I didn't get up, he walked out of the kitchen. I stared after him, feeling a little deflated. For a minute there I thought he might be a little different than everyone else. Guess I was wrong.

Seconds later he returned, with a set of car keys in his hand. "You coming?" he asked and snagged his can off the table beside me.

I stood up quickly and he smiled. It was a knowing smile and I wanted to kick myself in my own ass. *Way to look desperate, Kelly.*

I was never desperate for anything and if I was, I never, ever showed it.

So why is it that when this used-to-be friend turned geek-who-might-be-kinda-hot turned up with a set of car keys I tripped over myself to follow him out the door?

"Get your notebook, Kel," he said, fondness in his tone.

He hasn't called me that in years.

I backtracked to grab my notebook and pencil off the table, Eric was already out of the kitchen and heading through the mudroom on his way to the back door.

It wasn't until I was rushing after him that I realized I was carrying school supplies to do an assignment and chasing after a geek.

And I wasn't bored.

In fact, I was actually kind of excited.

Chapter EIGHT

Legit – saying something is legitimate.

Eric

ONE MINUTE I was trying to avoid her, snapping at each other in the kitchen… then the next she was sitting in the passenger seat of my mom's Buick and I was in the driver's seat.

I don't know what I was thinking.

I kinda felt bad about being an ass to her in the kitchen after school. I'd been pissed at my dad, pissed at the stupid pipes in my house, and I took it out on her.

She deserved it, but still.

Kelly always looked so shocked when I rebuffed her or snapped back. The look on her face the day we moved in and I slammed the door in her face, it was sort of epic. Everybody always did what she wanted and if they didn't, she could manipulate or punish them.

That wasn't going to work with me. She was beginning to see that, and I had to admit, watching her come to terms with it was pretty amusing. I also kind of liked the way her eyes sometimes flared when I did something she didn't expect.

Like earlier when I refused to move. Or when I sat down at the table beside her.

I liked getting a reaction out of Kelly. I liked it when she looked at me as if I was an equation she wanted to figure out.

Never in a million years did I think I'd be sitting in a car alone with her. If someone had told me even last week this would be happening, I would have offered to drive them to the mental ward.

Here we were. The streets were already dark, but her golden hair was sort of like its own light. I had to fight to keep my eyes ahead and not allow them to drift to where she sat.

She smelled good. It was probably all the hairspray in her hair, but I liked it just the same. She'd changed her clothes since school. She was wearing bright blue leggings, yellow socks that climbed partway up her calves, and a yellow t-shirt that ended as the waistband of the pants started. The shirt was loose, so it kept falling down over her shoulder, exposing the creamy skin there.

There was nothing beneath her shirt. No bra strap, no tank top. That meant her bare chest was rubbing up against her shirt…

"Where are we going?" she asked.

I cleared my throat and focused on the road. "Almost there," I replied.

"This is your mom's car right?" she asked.

I glanced over at her. "No. I stole it from the neighbor."

"Not funny." She threw me a look, but her glossy lips pulled into a rueful smile.

"Remember when she use to take us for ice cream?" Kelly mused.

"You always got extra cherries," I said.

"You remember that?" She seemed surprised.

"I remember lots of things."

We both fell silent. I took the next turn and drove down the street and pulled into the parking lot. Through the window, Kelly stared up at the stone building even after I shut off the engine.

"What is this place?" she asked, suspicion in her tone.

"You don't trust me?" I asked.

She turned the full voltage of her blue eyes on me. "Do you trust me?"

I once did.

I still wanted too.

But I wasn't sure if I should.

"It's a planetarium," I answered.

"We have a planetarium in this town?" She seemed shocked.

I guess since it isn't beside the mall, she wouldn't have seen it. I kept that little joke to myself. She probably wouldn't be as entertained by it as I was.

"So what do you say?" I asked. "Want to go inside and have a little constellation lesson?"

"Beats reading the textbook."

"Words every guy wants to hear," I muttered as I got out of the car.

She met me in front of the hood a funny look on her face.

"What?" I asked.

"Do you date much?"

I couldn't help it. I laughed, but it wasn't because I was amused. "What's the matter, hard to think a girl would date someone like me?"

"I didn't mean to offend you." She almost sounded contrite.

"This way," I instructed as we entered the building and I headed toward a set of stairs. It was dark in here. The community building was already closed for the evening and everyone was gone for the day.

"This is creepy," she said from behind and I felt her brush against the back of my arm. I glanced over my shoulder.

Kelly was practically pressed against me.

I stopped abruptly. "You hear that?"

She was so close she ran right into me when I stopped. Her entire body came in to contact with mine. She made a low shrieking noise and I lifted my arm to wrap around her.

"What noise?" Her eyes rounded, looking like huge, white orbs in the dark. She clung to me. I don't even think she realized it, but I did.

Oh, did I ever.

"Nothing," I said and smiled.

She made a sound and yanked back to punch me in the stomach. "You did that on purpose!"

I laughed. "I couldn't resist. Still afraid of the dark, I see."

"I'm leaving," she sniffed, and turned to rush to the door.

I caught her hand. "What about your assignment?"

She glanced down at where our hands held, then back up at me. In that moment, she looked a lot like the girl I use to know. Except, you know older now.

She seemed unsure, but with her hand in mine it was like it used to be. I was the brave one back then, I was the one who took care of her.

"Planetariums are dark." Her teeth sunk into her lower lip.

"You really are still scared of the dark?" I asked, I tugged her and she took on step forward.

We were still holding hands and it kicked up some nerves in the pit of my stomach. Like this unsteady, shaky feeling deep down. This was new. This reaction to touching her had definitely not been there when we were kids.

"Yes and if you tell anyone…" she warned, the man-eater side to her coming out.

Man-eater side = the girl who takes what she wants without consequence. The girl who isn't afraid of anything.

But Kelly was afraid of the dark.

Maybe she wasn't such a man-eater after all…

"Chill. I won't ruin your precious popular girl status," I said. Usually this would have pissed me off, the "new" her on display. But it was hard to be mad when she was still holding my hand and it felt really good.

You know what else felt good?

Her body against mine when she fell into me.

"Why is it so dark in here?" she grumped.

"Building is closed."

"Then what the hell are we doing here?" she asked, glancing around like we were about to get arrested.

"There you go being boring again," I teased.

She gave me a withering look.

"I know the guy who runs the planetarium. He won't care I'm here."

"How do you know him?" she asked, narrowing her eyes.

"I come here all the time. I did a report last year for school."

She nodded slow. "Isn't the planetarium dark too?"

I smiled. "Not when all the stars are lit up."

Our eyes collided and she smiled back at me. We stood there for a few seconds just smiling at each other and I felt like a goof, but I also didn't look away.

"I'll let you hold my hand," I cajoled.

I used to say the very same thing to her when we were small and she didn't want to climb to the top of the tallest slide at the park.

It always worked then.

"Fine," she agreed, and I had to admit, surprise rippled through me. Her fingers tangled tighter with mine and she stepped right up to my side. "But only because you know the way and I don't want to trip and fall."

"Obviously," I said, and smothered a smile.

Even after all these years it appeared I might still like her.

I pushed that thought away and guided her up a steep flight of stairs to a closed and locked wooden door. She didn't say anything when I found the spare key and unlocked the space.

I pushed open the door, but the room was even darker than the stairs and hall. She hesitated. I held out my hand again and she gave hers immediately.

I think I could get used to holding her hand.

Just inside, I flipped on a dim light and the place lit up.

It was a round room. It always made me feel like I was in a tower. Half the room was filled with seats, each row a little bit higher than the one in front of it. The seating formed a half circle and filled up half of the room. In front of the seats was the area where the guide would introduce what he would be talking about that day, and there was a chalkboard with a several chalky erasers and half pieces of white chalk where he could draw out examples and make notes.

In the very back of the room was the projector that was set up to project the images on the wide, round ceiling.

I hadn't lied when I said I came here a lot. It was a good place to think. The lights would go out and the instructor would go on and on about what was overhead. In a way, his boring voice was soothing, and I could just let my mind wander or work out stuff that was bothering me.

Plus, no one from school ever came here, so it was sort of like my own special spot away from reality.

"Wow, this is kinda rad," Kelly said, letting go of my hand and stepping further inside to look around.

I shut the door quietly behind us and went to the projector. Neither of us said anything as I looked around for the slide I wanted. Once I found it, I slid it inside and made a few adjustments.

"Pick a seat," I told her, and went to turn off the light.

She sat in the front row and I smiled a little when her knee started bouncing with nerves because I was about to plunge the room into darkness.

"It won't be that dark for long," I promised.

She nodded and I hit the light.

"Eric?" she said after, like, ten seconds of pitch black.

I chuckled. "I'm still here, Kel. Hang on."

I felt around for the switch and flipped it on. Stars and planets lit up over head, turning the pitch black into a nighttime sky that was anything but scary.

"Whoa," she whispered. I could see the top of her head from where I was. It was upturned toward the ceiling and her face was illuminated softly from the lights overhead.

After I made sure all was right with the projector, I slid into a seat beside her. "What do you think?"

"It's so pretty."

I spent the next while pointing out constellations, giving her history and names. She was totally into it and when I started telling her the legends with the Gods and how the constellations came to be, her eyes lit up.

Who's the geek now? It was a dumb thought and I pushed it away. People might call me a geek, but I wasn't. Not at all. Just because I did well in school and wore glasses didn't make me somehow not as cool as say the jocks. Those guys were jerks.

Since I didn't like to be called a geek, it wouldn't be fair to call her one either.

I wondered what she would think about the label everyone had given her? I knew she didn't know about it. If she did, she'd probably throw a fit.

"How do you know all this stuff?" she asked, still gazing up at the stars.

"I'm just making it all up," I deadpanned.

She jerked back and stared at me. Her mouth formed a little o and it drew all my attention to her forever pink lips. "Seriously?"

"Your face right now," I teased and couldn't resist using my finger to push the bottom of her chin up so her mouth closed.

The death glare was back on her face again. "If I get a bad grade on this…"

"You'll what? Tell everyone I'm a geek?"

Her face changed. She actually looked a little sad. "I don't make the rules of high school."

"You just follow them," I said, glancing away.

"Don't we all?" Her voice was soft, imploring me to understand.

But I didn't. I didn't understand why people had to change. Why people had to turn their backs on people they were supposed to love.

"I was just kidding before. Everything I told you," I cleared my throat, "about the stars is true."

"I believe you," she whispered and looked back up at the stars.

I felt fidgety suddenly, so I got up and went back to the projector to change some of the views. It was more comfortable to fall into the role of tutor I made sure to change the sky so it was mottled with different colors and light. Kelly seemed enraptured by that part the most.

I guess I should have known—some of the sky was pink, and that seemed to be her favorite color.

I went on, talking more and switching out the slide. We didn't talk much other than for her to point out things she thought were interesting so I could talk about them.

"That should be enough for you to write a two-page summary for class," I said, switching back to the view I'd originally turned on. I liked this one the best. It was a little darker than the others, and the stars came through more clearly because the backdrop was colorless.

"We're done?" she asked, turning in her chair and peering over the back toward where I stood.

"Yeah."

"Can we stay a little longer?" she asked, surprising me. "I like it here."

"Sure." I left the projector and wandered back to where she was sitting, but I didn't sit back down. It was kind of hard to sit beside her.

"Tell me about that one again," she asked, pointing up.

I smiled. That one would be her favorite. She always had liked fairy tales.

"That's Andromeda," I explained for the second time tonight. "She was a princess, daughter of Cepheus and Cassiopeia."

Without taking her eyes off the constellation, she patted the seat beside her. I paused, wondering if she realized what she had done.

Because I was no longer talking, she glanced over and motioned for me.

I gave in. Maybe I wasn't so immune to the man-eater's charms after all.

I stretched my legs out in front of me when I sat down and looked up instead of at her (even though I wanted to look at her).

"Andromeda's mother had a big head and she use to tell anyone and everyone that would listen that her daughter was the most beautiful of everyone. Even the Nereids."

"Think she was?" Kelly interrupted. As she spoke, she linked her arm with mine, and leaned her cheek on my shoulder.

My legs pulled in, my feet flattened on the floor. Kelly didn't move. She just sat there, almost snuggled against me, staring up at the sky.

My heart rate doubled in seconds. The scent I had noticed in the car wafted over me once more.

"Eric?" she murmured.

"Uh, I'm not sure," I said. "I think her mother was probably a little biased."

She laughed lightly. "Most moms are."

I nodded even though she wasn't looking at me. I could barely think with her lying on me like this. "Poseidon was angered by her mother's claims, and in a wrath sent a sea monster to devour Andromeda. She was chained to the rocks about to become dinner when Perseus saw her. He thought she was very beautiful as well and battled the sea monster."

"And then he carried her off and made her his wife," Kelly ended and sighed.

I glanced down at her. With her face upturned, I could see all of it. Her eyes looked dreamy—like the story entranced her—and her skin sort of sparkled beneath the low light.

She was beautiful. She always had been.

"That's so romantic." She smiled, her eyes changing direction and looking up at me.

I swallowed thickly. "You still like fairytales."

"You seem surprised."

"A lot about you surprises me, Kel."

"You were the only one who's ever called me that."

My eyes bounced between hers. I felt so pulled to her. She was familiar yet new to me all at the same time. I'd never felt anything like that before.

She broke eye contact first, but didn't pull away. She stayed against my shoulder, her arm linked with mine and her hand curled around my forearm like she'd sat this way a million times before.

Her cheek felt warm against my shoulder, even through the fabric of my shirt.

"It's like we aren't even in Bakers Town anymore. Like we're in our own little universe," she mused, glancing around.

"Do you like it here?" I asked. Instantly, I wanted to kick my own ass. What the hell was I thinking asking her that? Of course she'd rather be in Bakers Town. She was practically the reigning queen.

Her cheek moved against me, her face tipped back up. "I do."

She meant it. I could see the truth right there in her eyes.

In that moment everything fell away. Who she was. Who I was. Who we used to be.

I leaned in, bringing my face inches away from hers. I felt the change in her. She knew what I wanted to do. I expected her to shove away and shriek.

She didn't.

She waited, the tips of her fingers tightened on my arm.

The hell with it.

I swooped in and pressed my lips against hers. My eyes stayed open long enough to watch hers sweep closed.

It felt like a firework went off inside me. Light burst behind my eyes and my mouth started to move. I kissed her deeply because that's the way I wanted to kiss her. I took charge of her mouth and our kiss. My lips ground against hers. The taste of her lipstick hit my tongue and I kissed harder.

My tongue tentatively stroked across hers, measuring the way she would react. She froze for a fraction of a second, then opened further and I thrust my tongue inside to stroke over hers.

Too many people treated her like she was in charge. Too many people gave her all the power.

Not me. Not this kiss.

This kiss was mine.

I'd share it with her, but on my terms.

Her nails dug into my forearm and her body leaned further into mine. I kept my hands where they were, even though I was dying to touch her.

I wanted her to want me. I wanted her to know what it was like to lack.

With one last stroke of my tongue I broke the kiss.

She gasped and sat back, her face full of shock. "You kissed me."

"You liked it."

Kelly practically jumped out of the seat and clutched her notebook in front of her. "We should go."

Without another word, I got up and shut the projector down. With it off, the room plunged into absolute blackness. I could hear her breathing as I made my way back over to where she was standing.

"C'mon." I felt for her hand.

"You could have waited 'til I was at the door to turn off all the lights," she said as I guided us.

"I could have," I agreed. "But then you wouldn't hold my hand."

"Eric…" she whispered.

Annoyance pinched my chest. I knew what that meant. I knew the hesitant, almost warning sound to her voice.

I pushed open the door and busied myself with locking up.

I didn't reach for her hand again as we went down the stairs and through the hall to the exit. She stayed close though, and as annoyed as I was, I couldn't bring myself to move away. She was scared and this was probably the last time I'd ever be close like this with her again.

Outside the air was a lot cooler, nightfall in full swing. The Buick wasn't parked far, but even so, out of the corner of my eye I saw Kelly shiver. I looked over completely in time to see her hardened nipples press against her top before she wrapped her arms across her chest.

I couldn't stop my mind from wondering about what her bare chest would look like before me, open for my touch.

She went ahead and got in the passenger seat but I went around to the trunk and reached in for what I wanted. After I closed it, I stood at the bumper and let the cold air sink in because I was getting too hot.

One kiss, and I was thinking about her naked chest and what it would be like to run my hands and mouth all over her body.

Shaking off the thoughts, I walked around to her side and pulled open the door.

"What are you doing?" she asked, alarmed.

"Here," I said and thrust my jean jacket at her. "It's pretty cold out."

I tried and failed miserably not to look at her chest. Her nipples were still totally hard and looked like rocks beneath her shirt.

"Thanks," she said, and reached for my jacket.

By the time I got into the driver's side, she was wearing it and I wondered why I had to be a gentleman, because giving her that jacket totally ruined my view.

We didn't say anything at all on the ride back to her house. When I parked in the driveway and shut off the engine, she turned toward me. "Thanks for helping me with the assignment."

"No problem."

"Uh, about what happened…" she began.

"You mean when I kissed you?" I said.

She nodded and ducked her head.

"What about it?" I wasn't going to make this easy. Now that the night was over I was feeling even more annoyed.

"We just… we got caught up with the story, and the stars… it shouldn't have happened."

"Right." My voice was tight.

"If you could not tell anyone about it,"

"Don't worry," I snapped, cutting her off. I didn't want to hear any more of her rejection. "I won't tell anyone I kissed you and you liked it."

She stiffened. "Who said I liked it?"

"I still have the nail marks on my arm to prove it," I half growled.

"Maybe I was trying to pry you off me!"

"If that's what you gotta tell yourself, Kel," I chuckled, but it was a mean, hard sound.

"Don't call me that!" she huffed and threw the door open and leapt out into the driveway.

"No?" I called after her as she stripped off my jacket. "Maybe I should call you what everyone else does, then!"

The jacket flew in the door, across the seats, and slapped me in the face.

She did not just do that.

I grabbed a fistful of the material and yanked it down ready to yell some more.

But she was already gone.

Fled back into the house.

Back into the universe where she was everything and I was just a geek.

Chapter NINE

Chill – a way to tell someone to calm down.

Kelly

I RUSHED UP to my room and shut the door. Leaning against it, I pressed my fingers against my lips.

They were tingling.

Still.

I had no idea he could kiss like that. I had no idea anyone could kiss like that.

It unsettled me. It shook me. It ate away at me…

I never should have allowed it to happen, but unlike I led people to believe, I was only a girl. And not a very strong one at that.

If I was as strong as everyone thought, well…

I shook off the thought.

Images of the way Eric looked sitting there beside me with the sky all lit up flashed in my head. I leaned a little heavier into the door.

Why hadn't I noticed how adorably sexy he was before?

The curls on his head, the glasses, and his soulful brown eyes… gah!

And the sound of his voice. It was almost like I was hypnotized as he told me myth after myth of the constellations. The stories were tragic and beautiful all at once. It made looking up at the stars even more romantic.

His shoulder was just as strong as it looked. I simply could not resist leaning into him as he spoke. I felt like the moon he spoke of, circling the earth. I was the moon and he was the earth; I rotated around his voice until I was completely pulled in.

Eric was the only one who knew I was afraid of the dark.

I'd told him back before I'd known enough to be self-conscious. He'd never laughed at me back then and he hadn't laughed tonight. He'd offered to hold my hand.

Just like back then, I couldn't resist. There was something so basic about us when we were together. Like we belonged together.

When I was small and innocent, I called it friendship.

Now?

Now I called it scary.

I was so scared I hurt him. I saw it flash in his eyes back there in the car. I'd basically told him I hadn't wanted to kiss him, that I hated it.

It was a total lie.

But a necessary one.

Eric and I were the past.

Used-to-be-friends. He was the one who ended it, and I knew now it was for the best. We were from two different circles. We would never work.

I could never walk down the hall at school holding his hand.

It would be social suicide.

Soon, he would go back to his house and I could go back to pretending I never saw him.

Out in the hallway, I heard the distinct opening and closing of his bedroom door.

My hand wrapped around the doorknob before I realized what I was doing and forced myself to stop. Apologizing would only make things worse.

I decided to distract myself with writing my report while everything he'd taught me tonight was fresh in my mind. I laid across my bed and wrote it all out, finishing the paper completely.

As I was getting ready for bed, I felt a sense of accomplishment for completing the entire assignment in just one night.

I credited my enthusiasm to get it done with my need for a distraction.

As I laid in bed and listened for any muffled sounds coming from his room, I felt sort of sad. That's when I realized I hadn't been distracting myself at all with that paper. I'd used it as an excuse.

An excuse to stay in that little universe we'd been in when we kissed just a little bit longer.

I refused to look at him in school and skipped dinner the next night. Sitting at the table with him and pretending everything was normal was impossible.

I didn't know how to act around him anymore.

Up until the planetarium, it was easy to stay on my side of the invisible line between us. Having him around reminded me of when we were little, and it made me curious. I wondered who he was now, but I also wondered what happened all those years ago when he pulled away from our friendship.

That line between us, though invisible, became almost non-existent as we sat under the stars in his planetarium and I listened to the sound of his voice filling up the star-soaked darkness.

That kind of thing changed a girl.

Or maybe it just brought out the real me.

I don't know. I was confused.

All I knew is that one minute a line was drawn, and the next he totally stepped over it and was kissing me like no one ever kissed me before.

Eric kissed like he owned my lips. Like he had every right to kiss me and stoke his tongue right over mine.

No one had ever acted like that before. Most guys were more cautious, like they weren't sure how far they could go with me. Like they were intimidated.

Eric was not intimidated by me.

Just in the past few days, he'd challenged me. When we kissed I'd felt like I was a wild horse and he was the gentle, yet commanding, hand that tamed me.

I couldn't just sit at the dinner table with a guy like that.

He made me nervous and excited, but it didn't matter. Girls like me didn't date boys like him. I didn't date anyone, really. I flirted, played games, and got guys interested. I let them think they had a chance – no, *more* than a chance with me.

Then I dropped them.

Game over.

Harsh? Maybe.

I'd learned the past couple years it was better that way. I was only doing what lots of guys did. They liked the thrill of the hunt, they liked the chase. Once most had a girl good and hooked, they moved on.

And the girls?

They needed a lesson in who was at the top. A lot of girls were fine with where they fell in the high school hierarchy. They had their group of friends, just like I had mine. I waved and smiled at them almost daily because they weren't my enemies. We co-existed in a good place. In a neutral place.

But then there were the other girls… the ones whose eyes you felt drilling a hole into your back. The ones who paid attention with hawk-like attention to everything I wore, said and did. They had their eyes on my spot. The top spot.

They would overthrow me if they could and not think twice.

Most people wanted to be me, but there were some who thought they actually had a shot at it.

Those were the girls who needed reminding. They needed to be put not so subtly back in their place.

Taking their boyfriend or die-hard crush was my way of doing that.

The loud sound of the phone broke into my thoughts. The shrill sound of its ring echoed up the stairs. A few seconds later, my mother yelled up the stairs.

"Kelly! You have a phone call!"

I bounced down the stairs and picked up the receiver, which Mom had balanced on top of the portion hanging on the wall.

"Hello?" I said and twisted the cord around my finger.

"I have no idea what to wear," Mandy said into my ear.

"We went shopping," I said and rolled my eyes. "You got an outfit."

"I got two and now I can't decide!" she burst out.

I smiled at the phone. She was so erratic. I always dressed fashionably and I loved clothes just as much as Mandy, but she tended to be more indecisive whereas I was quicker to settle on something. Maybe it was because I rocked everything.

"Wear the dress," I said. It was totally in right now with its tighter skirt and big poufy sleeves. It had a heart shaped neckline so she could wear a necklace or something with it.

"It is Tad's favorite color," she agreed.

The mention of Tad made my stomach drop. I'd actually totally forgotten about him. "I didn't know blue was his favorite," I said to keep the conversation going.

I so did not want to think about Tad.

"He's been so weird lately."

"Oh," I said, twirling the cord a little bit tighter around my finger. "How?"

"Distant, kind of moody. He didn't even call me last night!"

"Guys are so weird," I murmured.

"So yeah," she went on. "Totally the blue."

"Totally," I echoed.

"Well, I better go. My hair is a mess and I want to be ready when Tad gets here to pick me up."

"Ok," I said, staring at my feet.

"We'll be by not long after to get you," she added.

I forgot they were driving me! It was just another excuse to be around Tad, but now I didn't want to be around him at all.

I wrapped an arm across my stomach. "No, I'll meet you there. It will give you and Tad some alone time. Sounds like you need it."

"Thanks, Kelly. You're a good friend."

I wanted to gag. "See ya later," I said, and quickly hung up the phone.

Mandy didn't deserve this. She didn't deserve me snatching Tad right out from under her. She liked him and I was ruining that. I knew what it was like when you liked someone and then suddenly they just weren't around anymore.

Why had I thought this was a good idea? Why had I thought she deserved this? She wasn't one of those girls that needed a lesson… she was my best friend.

Why was I suddenly having a change of heart now?

"You girls make your plans for tonight?" my mom asked as she came into the room. She had blond hair just like me. She wore hers in a shorter style, but it was still fashionable. Her eyes were blue like mine as well. A lot of times people thought we were sisters and not mother and daughter.

"Yep," I replied. "Going to the mall. Might check out a movie."

"Sounds fun," Mom said. "You're staying over at her house, right?"

"I'm not sure," I said, even though that was the plan. Suddenly I didn't feel like partying so much.

"Is everything all right?" she asked.

"Totally," I said. "Mandy just got in a fight with Tad."

"Young love," Mom sighed with a faint smile.

"Mom?" I asked.

"Hmm?"

"What's love feel like?"

She smiled. "Well, it's sort of a whole mix of emotions at first. Like a nervous, excited feeling. When you see him, your heart beats a little faster and you forget where you are. You think about him all the time even when you know you should be thinking of other things."

"Is that how it is with you and Dad?"

"It was years ago. Now it just feels like happiness, like my life wouldn't be complete without him."

I nodded. I don't know why, but my chest felt a little tight. I also felt heavy with dread... I'd felt some of those things she just described. I'd felt them very recently.

"Is there a special someone in your life?" Mom asked.

I forced a laugh. "No. Unless you count myself."

Mom laughed lightly. "Focusing on yourself is always a good thing," she replied. "Just remember not to become too self-centered, because then you sometimes miss what is right in front of you."

I stared at her, trying to figure out what she meant. Was she talking about Eric in a roundabout way?

"Right," I said. "Well, I better go get ready."

Halfway to the door I remembered I told Mandy not to pick me up. "Oh, can I borrow the car tonight?"

"I don't see why not," Mom replied.

"Thanks!" I spun back to the door and collided with Eric's chest. A sound escaped from my throat.

His hands gripped my arms to steady me. "Whoa."

My mouth ran dry and even though I wanted to yell at him for being in my way, I couldn't find the words. They just weren't there. He didn't release me right away. Instead, he looked into me with those light brown eyes. It felt invasive, like he saw deep down, saw more than I wanted him to see.

"Where are you going in such a hurry?" he asked, finally pulling his hands off me.

He didn't move though, he stayed there within inches of me, totally blocking the door.

My stomach bounced around at the sound of his voice. All I could think about was the way it sounded in the dark when he was speaking only to me.

"Uh," I stuttered. "I'm, ah, going out with friends."

"What are you doing tonight, Eric?" Mom interjected.

"I was supposed to go to a friend's, but those plans fell through."

"Oh no, what happened?"

"His mom happened," Eric said, totally amused.

I had no idea what that meant.

"Moms can be such a pain," my mom said, like she totally knew.

I looked at him and rolled my eyes.

He smiled softly and my heart rate doubled.

Oh shit. Not again.

I was experiencing all those things my mom just told me about love. With Eric.

No. No. No.

"Hey!" Mom said. "I have an idea. Kelly, take Eric with you tonight! Then he won't be here alone."

The room tilted. I was not taking Eric out with me tonight. No way in hell.

"Oh, he'd be totally bored. It's just a bunch of girls," I scoffed.

"I thought Tad was going?" Mom said.

Oh my God, had she heard my conversation?

She was totally eavesdropping!

"Well yeah," I hedged.

"He might like another man to hang out with," she glanced at Eric and winked.

It made me want to barf.

I gave Eric a *help me* look, but he just smiled like he was enjoying this. He was totally gonna pay for this later.

"Tad and Eric don't really know each other, Mom," I said. "We have different friends."

"All the more reason to bring Eric along! Introduce him around, make some new friends."

"I don't think Eric would have a good time," I said.

"You don't like the mall and the movies?" Mom asked Eric with raised brows.

"I love movies. Especially scary ones. They're even better in the *dark* theatre."

Was he goading me? Was he totally teasing me about my fear of the dark?

"What movie are you going to see, Kel?" Eric asked with a smirk.

He knew I wasn't going to see a movie, the rat! I'm sure he'd heard about the party everyone was going to. Was he mad he wasn't invited, or was he just trying to make me squirm?

"I'm not sure," I said giving him a death glare. "Probably a romance."

"What else are you going to do tonight, Eric?" Mom said. God, was she still here?

"I'll probably get a head start on next week's reading," he replied.

"It's settled. Kelly, if you want to borrow my car then you're going to take Eric with you to meet your friends."

"But," I started to protest.

"Oh, no," Eric jumped in. Maybe he finally realized this wasn't funny. "That's okay, Mrs. Ross, I'd rather stay home."

"But we're all going out. A friend of ours is having a surprise birthday party for her husband. Your mother is coming with us. I don't like the idea of you being here alone."

"I've been alone before," he said, an edge to his voice.

I glanced at him.

"Well not tonight." I knew that tone. There was no way I was getting out of here tonight without him. "Kelly?"

"Yes, ma'am," I mumbled.

Mom smiled. "Good. When you are both ready, come see me and I'll give you the keys."

Eric and I both scattered from the room like leaves on a windy day. If we hung around any longer, there was no telling what she'd do. Halfway up the stairs I tossed him an evil look over my shoulder then stomped the rest of the way up.

In the hallway in front of our rooms, I swung to face him. "You just had to tell her you had no plans."

"How was I supposed to know she'd do that?" he shrugged.

"So what?" I whisper-yelled. "I'm supposed to just show up with you at Aaron's party?"

"That would be, like, totally embarrassing," he mocked me with a stubborn glint in his eye.

I sighed. I wasn't trying to hurt his feelings. I stared at him trying to figure out what to do.

"Relax," he finally said. "I'll leave with you so you can get the car and you can just let me off around the block and I'll walk back here and sneak up to my room."

"Really?" I asked, relieved.

"I have no desire to be seen with someone who doesn't want to be seen with me." His voice was tight.

"Eric." I was a horrible person. First I betrayed my best friend and now this…

"Just knock on my door when you're ready and we'll go downstairs," he said, and then disappeared into his room.

I stared after him a while, trying to figure out how all this happened.

It didn't bode well for the rest of my night.

Chapter TEN

Bombdigity – A way to say you really like something. Its like saying *Bomb,* but on steroids.

Eric

I NEVER CARED ABOUT ANY OF THIS STUFF.
I didn't want to be part of the in-crowd, or go to parties. That stuff was here today and gone tomorrow. It didn't last, so really, what did it matter?

Then Kelly knocked on my bedroom door.

Just seeing her standing there opened the floodgates for feelings I wasn't accustomed to.

Frustrated.

Angry.

Jealous.

It wasn't surprising that she looked beautiful. Kelly was the prettiest girl in the entire school. Honestly, she was the prettiest girl I'd ever seen.

Tonight her hair was pulled up into some kind of side ponytail, high on her head. The bangs at the front were teased up like all the girls wore and the scrunchie holding the hair in place around her ponytail was black, a direct contrast to her blond hair.

The make-up she wore looked like it usually did, not too much but enough to enhance her face, especially her blue eyes. But tonight her lips weren't pink like they usually were. They were red. Bold, bright red that coated the fullness of her lips and made me remember exactly what it had been like to kiss her.

She was wearing a body hugging black skirt and a wide leopard print belt with a huge buckle in the center. The black shirt had sleeves, but was off the shoulders. The shirt, coupled with her pulled up hair, left a lot of skin to the eye.

For the first time ever, I wanted to be part of the in-crowd.

For the first time ever, jealousy spewed up the back of my throat like the cafeteria ladies' mystery lunches.

"What are you wearing?" she gasped looking at me.

"I was just about to ask you the same thing."

The surprised look I was starting to get used to seeing on her face appeared. "What's wrong with what I'm wearing?"

"It shows too much skin," I blurted out.

She made a face. "It's the style."

"I don't like it."

She crossed her arms over her chest and glared at me. "Well your outfit looks… stupid!"

I lifted an eyebrow. "That's the best you can do?"

"Shut up," she snapped. Her hand pressed against my chest and she walked forward, shoving me back into my room.

"What are you doing?" I asked.

"If you want to make them actually think you are going out with me and my friends then you have to dress like it."

"I go out like this all the time," I said, looking down at my pants and plain t-shirt.

"Exactly," she muttered, like that was some kind of argument.

"Where's all your clothes?" she asked, going through all the empty drawers in the dresser. Like I'd bother to unpack. We were going home soon.

"In my bags over there."

She went over and started going through all my stuff.

"Sure, help yourself," I remarked dryly.

"You need help," she retorted.

I admit, I didn't argue as much as I usually would because she was bent over my things and giving me a really nice view of her ass.

That skirt hugged all the right places.

Which is exactly why she shouldn't be wearing it.

"I look fine," I grunted. "Let's go."

"Put this on," she said, handing me a plain white t-shirt.

"It's the same thing I'm wearing now, but a different color," I said, staring at it.

"I like it better," she sniffed.

"Fine." I snatched it out of her fingers. Clearly we weren't getting out of here until I changed.

I yanked the faded blue shirt over my head and tossed it on the bed.

She made a sound and I glanced up. She was staring. I lowered my hands to my sides and let her look.

"Like something you see?" I asked.

She spun around with a huffing sound.

I grinned at her back and pulled on the shirt. "What about the jeans?" I said, gesturing to my faded denim.

"They'll do," she said.

On the foot of the bed was the jacket I'd let her borrow on the way home from the planetarium. She scooped it up and held it out. "Here."

I shrugged it on and started toward the door.

"Wait," she caught my hand and I stopped instantly. I looked down, staring at where we touched.

Touching her now was more exciting than when we first touched. Now I knew what it felt like, I knew how my nerve endings sizzled beneath my skin.

"Your hair." She released my hand and stepped up close.

She smelled good… like hairspray and perfume.

Her fingers delved into my hair and my vision went a little blurry. "What are you doing?" I asked, trying to sound annoyed.

I'm pretty sure I failed.

God, I liked when she touched me.

"You need a haircut," she fussed, pushing the curls that always fell onto my forehead up off my face.

If I got a haircut you wouldn't need to fix it, I thought. But all I said was, "No. I don't."

"That's better." She pulled back and I had an urge to shake my head and mess it all up again. "C'mon."

I followed her out into the hallway and down the stairs. Before we went in the kitchen she said, "Remember—mall and the movies."

I rolled my eyes. She acted like I was an idiot.

Course, maybe I was, going along with all this.

"Mom!" Kelly said. "We're ready to go."

Her parents and my mom weren't in the kitchen, so we went into the living room and they weren't there either. I trailed along behind her back out into the entry when all three of them came down the steps.

"Perfect timing!" her mom said. "We're just on our way out, too."

"Great," Kelly said. "Can I have the car keys?"

"Sure," her mom said and pulled them out of the bag hanging on her shoulder on a gold chain. "Here you go."

"Thanks."

"You two kids have fun tonight," her dad said.

"Yes, sir," I replied.

My mom smiled. "So good to see you too hanging out again!"

Kelly's dad opened the front door and held it for everyone. When Kelly didn't head outside, he glanced at her. "I just forgot something upstairs," she said. "You all go ahead. I wouldn't want you to be late."

I gave her a look. She was totally stalling so they would leave first and not see me stay home.

"We'll wait!" her mom called from outside.

Kelly made a show of running upstairs and then right back down. She patted her purse for the sake of it and then rushed outside.

I muffled a laugh when I noticed the car we were taking was blocking the one everyone else was piling in to.

Kelly climbed behind the wheel and I got in the passenger side. She backed out of the driveway and her father followed behind. When she pulled down the road, he followed right along behind her.

"So much for dropping me off the next street over," I mused.

Our parents followed us halfway to town before they finally turned off and left us on the road without a tail. "Finally," she muttered.

"You can just drop me off here," I said.

"No way!" she gasped. This is too far to walk. And it's dark out!"

"So?"

"So tons of kids just up and disappear these days. Haven't you seen the news?"

"I didn't know you worried about me."

Her eyes left the road for a second to look at me before glancing back on the road. "When we get to the party, you can just take the car and drive back to my house. I'll get a ride with Mandy and Tad."

"What if someone see's us!" I gasped.

"Shut up." She rolled her eyes.

"At least I look acceptable in this fresh outfit you picked out," I joked.

"Your hair is already falling in your face again," she complained, but there was a big smile on her face.

"You like it," I argued.

"Maybe I do."

"Was that a compliment?" I teased.

"No."

"I think it was." I grinned at her widely and she chuckled.

We turned onto a street of large houses with large green lawns. Between every house was a row of hedges that gave each yard some added privacy. Maybe that's why this guy's parties never got busted and parents never found out.

"So, why didn't you just have Mandy and Tad drive you tonight?" I asked.

"Guess I just felt like driving," she said, suddenly very interested in the road.

"Was it because of Tad?" I pressed.

Her hands tightened on the steering wheel. "Why would you think that?"

"C'mon, Kel, I'm not stupid," I said, irritated. "I have eyes. You've totally been hitting on him lately."

"Has it been that obvious?" she asked, a slight frown pulling at her red pout.

Well, yeah. Hence the nickname. "To me it has," I said. "But I pay attention."

"You must think pretty low of me," she whispered. The car slowed and I figured we were approaching the house. Cars were parked along the sides of the road, but they were scattered a bit so it didn't look so obvious someone was having a party.

I wasn't sure what to say. It seemed whatever I said would probably get me in trouble.

Luckily, I was saved from answering because she pulled to the curb and let the car idle. "I can walk from here."

"Which house is it?" I asked. Seemed I should be able to tell which one was the party house.

"It's a few up."

I shook my head. "No way. You aren't walking alone in the dark."

"There's people right up the block."

"No." I meant it. "It's not safe."

She measured me in the dark interior of the car for long moments, a challenge sparking in her eyes. I stared back and didn't blink.

Finally, she relented and looked away.

"You're bossy, you know that?"

"Not really, I just don't let you roll over me like everyone else."

"I don't roll over everyone," she snapped.

"Maybe I should ask Tad about that."

She jerked like I slapped her. I felt bad, but not enough to apologize. It kind of pissed me off she was getting out of this car and going into a party where he was. Where any guy was.

"I can't make anyone do anything they don't want too," she reasoned.

"I think you are probably pretty convincing."

"I'm getting out," she announced, anger behind the words. Kelly left the car running and flung open the door to vault out onto the pavement.

I muttered a curse, shoved open my door and stepped out onto the sidewalk. Her heels slapped against the road and then on the concrete as she stepped onto the sidewalk in front of me. She didn't even glance in my direction, but pivoted and practically marched away.

"No you don't," I said and caught her wrist, forcing her to stop.

She snatched her arm back and glared at me. "I'm going."

"Then I'll follow."

"It's just right up the street!" she exclaimed and flung out her arms. "Who cares?"

"I do," I growled low.

That shut her up. It shut me up too.

We stood there, glaring at each other, and I tried to make sense of the dynamic swirling between us. She made me so crazy. Crazier than I'd ever felt. Like no matter how long I tried, she was a puzzle that would never be solved.

She was smarter than this and it pissed me off she didn't seem to care.

I *kissed* her. Took her to *my* spot and she didn't seem to care.

"Just get in the car," I said finally. "I'll drop you in front of the house. No one will know it was me driving. After tonight we can go back to the way it's been for years. As if we don't even know each other."

The whites of her eyes grew larger and I thought for just a fraction of a second maybe she didn't like that idea. But then she glanced away. "Fine." Her voice was tight and low.

Because I didn't trust her not to run off in those clunky heels, I wrapped my hand around her arm, just above her elbow. My fingers almost touched and it kind of amazed me at how much bigger I was than her.

I guess she was just so large in personality and presence, sometimes I forgot I was the bigger one.

Surprisingly, she didn't try to pull back. Leading the way, I started down the sidewalk to where the car was still running.

I got maybe two steps.

Two figures materialized out of the dark in front of us.

"Kelly?" the girl said. She was wearing heels too and a dress with a ruffled skirt. It wasn't nearly as tight as Kelly's, and I wished Kelly was wearing that right now instead.

"Uh, hi, Rebecca. I didn't see you there," Kelly said, her voice surprised and wary. "Hey, Todd." She waved to the guy.

"Are you and Eric here together?" Rebecca asked. The disbelief, shock and underlying thrill in her tone made my back teeth come together.

"Well, uh," Kelly stuttered, trying to come up with something. She looked like a deer caught in a pair of headlights.

Bet she regretted trying to run off now.

"They're holding hands," Rebecca told Todd like we weren't standing here within earshot.

I wanted to roll my eyes. We weren't holding hands.

Kelly yanked her arm out of my grasp and laughed. "Stupid heels," she said. "You know how it is to try and walk in these things."

"Totally," Rebecca answered, her eyes bouncing between us.

There was a glint in her eye, like she'd found a pot of gold at the end of a rainbow.

"You and the science geek, huh?" Todd said.

"Yeah, that's me," I said abruptly. "The science geek, don't have an actual life outside of science or anything."

My sarcasm went right over Todd's head. Maybe it was because he got hit so much when he played football.

Or maybe he was just an idiot.

"He was helping me with my science extra credit," Kelly jumped in. "I totally bombed that pop quiz."

"Me too," Rebecca answered. "It was totally hard."

Todd nodded and I wondered if I was the only person who passed.

"But so, why are you here?" Rebecca asked, like she was confused. "Together."

It must be a permanent state for her.

Kelly faltered.

"Because I asked her to bring me," I said. "In exchange for helping her with her science. I asked her to get me in to a party. You know, since all I ever do is study. I wanted to see what a party was like."

"Tubular," Todd grinned. "Like a charity project."

I nodded because if I opened my mouth, something nasty was going to come out. Did these people really act like this all the time? I looked over at Kelly to see what she thought about me being her "charity project." She refused to look at me, choosing instead to look at her shoes.

"Let's get this party started!" Todd launched forward and slung his arm around my shoulders. "C'mon, dude you can walk with me. I'll find you a nice spot in the corner and you can watch and learn."

I glanced over my shoulder as Kelly ran around to shut the car off and drop the keys in her bag. She looked panicked and relieved all at once.

When she saw me looking, she mouthed the words "thank you."

I looked away.

I just lied for her. I'd pretty much sold myself out so she wouldn't have to tell people why I was really here.

She let me.

It didn't feel good.

In fact, it kinda felt like shit.

Chapter ELEVEN

Jam – to leave abruptly.

Kelly

I WASN'T PROUD OF MYSELF.
I was adamant no one know Eric was at my house, or that I even knew him. I was so close, so close to having it all blow up in my face. And at the biggest party of the year, no less.

But it didn't.

Eric could have totally ratted me out. Just seconds before we were spotted on the sidewalk he'd been angry at me, he said some things that hurt…

I couldn't even be mad about it though.

Because the things he said were true.

Still, he covered for me. He stood there and played his "role" as the science geek.

He wasn't a geek.

He wasn't less cool than anyone in The Choice.

If anything, he was better. Eric didn't have to pretend to be someone. He didn't have to put on an act every single day. He made no apology for who he was… and that guy was pretty great.

I'd seen so many glimpses of the Eric I used to know.

He was funny and kind. Smart and eager to learn. He was good at telling stories and he didn't laugh at my fear of the dark.

He was my friend.

Even when we weren't friends.

Even when I didn't deserve it.

I'd let Todd and Rebecca call him a charity case and insult him.

Since he came to stay at the house, I felt like I was viewing things from different eyes. The reality I lived in was much more skewed and cruel.

I didn't know what to do.

You know what to do, a voice inside me argued.

I shied away from that voice.

Everyone stared when we walked into the party with Eric under Todd's arm. The interest in every eye in the room was overwhelming.

Rebecca and Todd were together, so automatically Eric and I were paired up in people's minds.

I heard some giggling, and then it turned into full blown laughter.

The boom box was turned down real low as people stared.

Todd seemed to eat up the attention while I wanted to shrink into the shadows. I looked at Eric to gauge his reaction, but it was too hard to tell. His face was impassive. Almost bored.

"So, like," Todd yelled out over the crowded room. "If we get a dork drunk, will he still be able to do math?"

Everyone roared with laughter and people started chanting, "Drunk, drunk, drunk!"

"So, I have a question," Eric said. He didn't yell like Todd, but everyone heard. It was like they were waiting to see what he would say. "If a stoner gets drunk, will it make him smarter?"

I burst out laughing and Rebecca glared at me. I pressed my lips together, contrite.

"You calling me stupid?" Todd said, his whole laid back demeanor changing. His arm dropped away from Eric's shoulders and he settled into a challenging stance.

People in the room watched. I could see their hope a fight would break out.

"Just following your lead," Eric said. "Making a joke."

He didn't act threatened at all by Todd. It was as if he didn't notice the intimidating way Todd faced him.

I respected Eric, I don't think I realized how much. In fact, in this moment I respected him more than anyone else in this entire house.

Even myself.

"Dudes," Aaron said, breaking away from the crowd. Aaron was the jock having this party, so he was the man in charge. "You're bringing down my rager."

I hardly would call this party a rager, but whatever.

"Kelly brought someone who doesn't belong here," Rebecca said, tossing me a harsh look.

Aaron glanced at Eric and then at me. "You brought a geek to my party?"

"He's totally lame, man," Todd said.

I rolled my eyes. "Two seconds ago you wanted to have a beer with him."

"Geeks don't belong here," Rebecca snapped. "This party is for cool people."

"Then why are you here?" I retorted.

She gasped like I smacked her.

I wanted to.

"I was just on my way out," Eric said, turning for the door.

My stomach dropped a little. I didn't want him to go.

But he couldn't stay.

"Hey, you forgot something!" Todd called out.

Oh no.

Eric turned around.

"Watch out!" I shrieked.

My warning came too late, Todd was already swinging, payback for the insult Eric delivered. I should have seen it coming sooner. Todd couldn't just let that go. Not here. Not in a room full of people.

I understood that more than anyone. Guys paid back people with violence, but me? I paid people back with games.

Right before the punch hit, Eric swerved out of the way and grabbed Todd just above his fist. Adeptly, he twisted the arm around Todd's back at an awkward angle. Todd was rotated around so his back was to Eric and he faced the watching crowd. Eric yanked a little harder and Todd's knee's buckled.

He made a sound like he was in pain, his face screwed up in a grimace.

"Gotta be quicker than that," Eric said.

Todd surged up but Eric twisted harder and he cried out again.

"Chill," Eric said. "I'm on my way out." He shoved Todd forward, who fell onto his knees and shook out his arm.

"Get him!" Aaron yelled.

Some of the other jocks in the room started forward.

Oh shit. Eric clearly knew some self-defense, he might even be able to punch, but there was no way he could defend himself against half a team of pissed off jocks.

"Wait!" I said and leapt between Eric and the advancing group.

They stopped and stared at me.

"We didn't come here for a fight. We came here to party."

"First you bring him, and then you defend him!" Todd yelled.

"She's nothing but a traitor!" a new voice – a very familiar voice rang out.

Everyone turned around to see who was talking. A group of people parted and then Mandy appeared.

She was wearing the blue dress like we talked about on the phone, her lips candy pink and her hair looking super teased out.

"Mandy?" I said, thinking I was crazy for assuming that angry look on her face was for me.

"What's the matter, Kelly?" she spat. "Run out of guys in your own circle to chew up and spit out?"

"What?" I echoed. Shock rippled through me as my mind went blank and I tried to make sense of her words.

"Please!" she yelled. "Don't play stupid, everyone in this entire room knows exactly what I'm talking about."

I glanced around. Girls were all nodding and even some of the guys.

"Maybe we should go talk," I told her.

"We don't need to talk," she spat. "Just answer this one thing: Did you hit on Tad? Did you kiss him?"

All the blood drained from my face and pooled in the bottom of feet. I felt dizzy, unable to run away because my legs felt too heavy to lift.

"Mandy, no, I—" I whispered.

"Don't lie! He told me! He told me before we got here. I confided in you. I told you he was acting weird. It's because he was thinking of breaking up with me for you!"

Murmurs and voices rushed through the room. Though they were quiet sounds, they pressed into my ears like shrill screams and I wanted to slap my hands over my ears and run away.

"How could you?" she demanded. "We were best friends. I defended you. I knew what everyone says about you, but I didn't think you'd do it to me."

"What everyone says?" I said, blank.

"Kelly's nothing but a man-eater," Mandy said. "She chews up guys and spits them out."

My mouth fell open.

And of course, just at that moment Brett materialized out of the group. He was holding a beer and looking at me with hurt, but also disgust.

To add to my humiliation Tad appeared, and right beside him was Brandon.

I think Brandon's presence hurt the worst. I know I wasn't with him, like, forever, but I actually liked him. He wasn't part of this. If anything, he did to me what I....

My eyes flew to him. "Was I...?"

A glint came into his eye. "A lesson you never learned."

My vision went blurry. I blinked back the tears threatening to spill over. *I would not cry. I would not cry.*

"How many boyfriends have you stolen, Kelly? Five? Ten?" Mandy pressed on. "Have you even told Brett that you're done with him? Did you tell him you moved on to my boyfriend?"

This wasn't supposed to happen. It wasn't supposed to be like this.

"And now you've moved on to the geeks!" Mandy kept going. I glanced around to see Eric was still standing there, stopped near the door and watching everything with hooded eyes. "Have you no respect at all?"

"Man-eater!" a girl in the back yelled.

I recognized her. I stole her boyfriend last year.

A cup of beer came flying out of nowhere and hit the floor at my feet. Beer splashed up all over my ankles and I jerked back.

"I did you a favor!" I shrieked. "If you had been dating anyone worth it he wouldn't have been so easy to steal!"

"Man-eater!" someone else yelled.

"Get out, Kelly. No one wants you here," Mandy said coldly.

I glanced at Tad and he turned his back. Then I looked at Brett, but he shook his head and turned to leave.

I was being ostracized by my own friends. By my own peers.

They called me a man-eater.

I spun and fled from the room, pushing past a few people and rushing around Eric. I left the front door open when I flung it open and rushed into the yard.

Tears blurred my vision, my heels sunk into the grass. Halfway to the sidewalk I saw a huge group of people. They all turned to stare.

I couldn't face them. I couldn't face anyone right now.

I ran away, along the thick hedge on the side of the yard and into the dark cover of the backyard. That's how upset I was, I couldn't even be afraid of the dark.

In fact, I was thankful for it.

It gave me a place to hide.

Man-eater.

In the center of the grass sitting under a large tree was a roughly built fort. It was dark, but I was close enough to see that it appeared to be constructed out of scrap wood and nails.

It looked like heaven to me.

The door creaked when I opened it but I didn't hesitate. I rushed inside and let the door close me in.

I couldn't see much of what was inside. It was so dark, it was sort of like a cell with a dirt floor. A creepy feeling spider-crawled up the back of my neck because of how inky black it was in here, but in that moment my pain was worse than my fear. Tears finally spilled over my cheeks and a sob caught in my throat.

I felt along the wall as I moved, then slid down onto my butt in the dirt. My face buried itself in my hands and I let out the cries I was holding back.

Here I was. The most popular girl at school, who was apparently the most talked about and quite possibly the most hated.

I was sitting in a prison crying.

A prison of my own making.

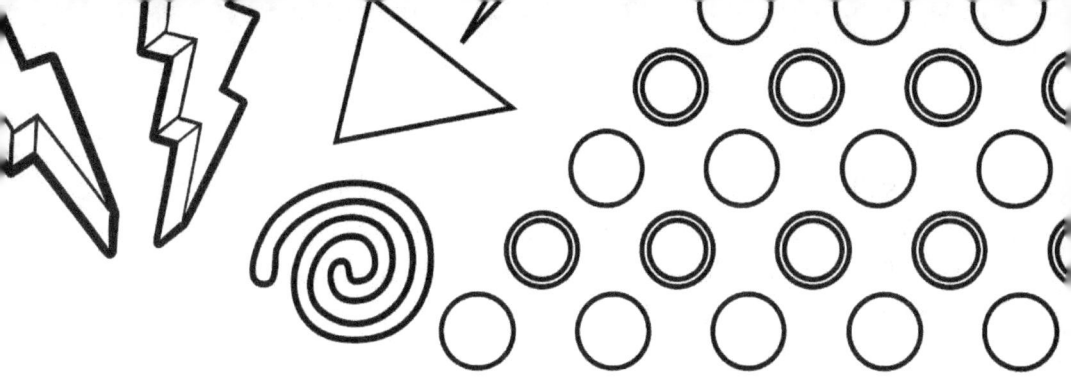

Chapter TWELVE

Whoa – when you are shocked, surprised, or any emotion really.

Eric

I CAN'T SAY I DIDN'T SEE THIS COMING.
Maybe not tonight. Maybe not in this way.

It had only been a matter of time until Kelly found out what everyone really thought of her.

Most would argue she deserved it. The head of that argument would be Mandy, Kelly's supposed best friend.

In fact, it seemed everyone in that entire room tonight thought Kelly deserved what was flung at her.

Except for me.

Even though she didn't speak up when they called me a charity case. Even though she refused to tell people I was staying at her house and that we used to be best friends. Even though she kissed me back but then refused to act like it mattered.

Like I mattered.

I still felt bad.

Maybe because as a "geek" I knew what it was like to get made fun of. Maybe I understood how it felt to be an outcast.

Or maybe it was just because I liked her.

Like *really* liked her.

Kelly did treat people not so good and she kinda did deserve that nickname. I don't think she deserved to be humiliated tonight.

I stepped out of the door not long after she did. The second she ran out, the party resumed, like nothing had happened at all.

I stared at Mandy for a few minutes before I went. She must have felt my stare because she glared back. Her glare didn't last though.

It slid away to reveal pain.

I don't know if it was pain from finding out her boyfriend wanted to ditch her for Kelly or pain that she'd just paid her best friend back in the worst way possible.

I couldn't help it.

The pain I saw in Mandy's eyes just wasn't enough.

She watched me approach and lifted her chin to meet my eyes.

"Feel better now?" I asked.

Anger snapped back over her features but she didn't agree. Because really, Mandy didn't feel better. I'd stand here and argue that she likely felt worse.

I leaned down beside her ear. "So tell me? How is what you did tonight any less worse than what she did to you?"

She sucked in a breath.

"Exactly," I whispered.

There was a crowd of people on the sidewalk. As soon as I saw them, I knew Kelly hadn't gone for the car.

The wind kicked up, pulling at my hair and clothes, as I walked toward the back yard. I glanced up at the sky. There was barely a single star in sight.

The sky felt low, like it was pressing down upon us. In the distance, a low rumble of thunder rolled through the night. Within minutes it would likely be raining.

The second I stepped behind the house, I knew where she'd gone.

I'd had a fort like this in my backyard when we were young. It was still there. It was weathered and beaten now, and I never went inside. Hell, most the time I avoided looking at it.

But I would never tear it down.

Kelly and I spent a lot of time in that fort. Playing games, eating Oreos and a secret stash of candy. She liked to draw on the wood walls with pink chalk. I wondered if I went inside if any of her markings would still be there.

Likely, some would be. But they'd be changed.

Just like the girl who put them there.

Another gust of wind shook the leaves overhead as I ducked inside the door. "Kelly?"

"Go away." Her voice was thick with tears and her nose sounded stuffy.

"I can't. You're my ride."

She made a choked sound and started crying more.

I shuffled from foot to foot and looked at her huddled shape in the dark. I probably wouldn't be able to see her at all if wasn't for all her blond hair.

Thunder boomed overhead and shook the sky.

Even though it was loud, I heard Kelly shriek and saw her jump.

"It's gonna storm," I said.

Duh.

I stepped close and towered over her. "C'mon, let's go before it starts."

Another loud clap of thunder smacked through the sky and she jolted again.

I sat down close beside her, so she was sitting sideways between my legs.

"I don't want to go out there." Her voice was muffled against her arm because her head was dipped into it.

The first splattering of raindrops slapped against the roof of the fort, sounding like they weighed a thousand tons. They were followed seconds later by a heavy downpour that pounded against the wood structure as the wind continued to blow.

Muted shrieks from people out in the front yard echoed, and I imagined everyone was running for the inside of the house.

"You knew what they all called me," she accused.

"It's not exactly a secret."

"Was to me," she muttered.

"Can you honestly say you didn't know people whispered and talked? That everyone stared at you because of more than just your clothes?"

"I thought they were just jealous."

"And now that you know differently?" I asked.

She started crying again. I didn't like to hear her cry. I liked it so much better when she smiled.

On impulse I reached out and she leaned toward me. I scooted just a little closer and held her against my chest. She buried her face in the crook of my arm and continued to cry.

The rain didn't let up at all. The sound of it drowned out most of the sounds she made, but I felt her shaking against me. Every so often, thunder would rumble and she would scoot just a little bit closer into my body.

I liked it.

A short while later, she lifted her head and looked up at me. Her makeup smeared in heavy rings around her eyes and streaked down her creamy cheeks. She kinda looked like a raccoon, but I didn't think she'd appreciate that observation so I didn't point it out.

"Why aren't you mad like the rest of them?" she asked, her voice hoarse. "You deserve to be."

Another strong gust of wind blew and the little fort rocked with it. The whites of Kelly's eyes grew larger and she glanced around nervously.

Pulling back from her slightly, I slid my jean jacket off. As I wrapped the coat around her shoulders and pulled it close beneath her chin, I said, "Were you really going to stop them tonight, you know, from beating me up?"

I thought about the way she'd jumped right in between me and the jocks, like she alone could stop what a group wanted to do.

She nodded. "I never should have let it get even that far. I should have stood up for you the minute Todd started acting like a jerk. I shouldn't have let him drag you in to the party… I shouldn't have let them make fun of you."

"You did though."

"I'm so sorry, Eric."

"You saying that because you really mean it, or because you just got treated the same way?" I asked.

"Both." Her shoulders sank. "I felt bad about it the entire time, but still I didn't say anything. I was too scared. Scared they'd…"

"Treat you the same?"

She nodded and more tears fell down her cheeks.

"I got so caught up in being the most popular. In being the girl everyone wanted me to be. I was good at it too, so good I lost myself. I became someone I didn't really want to be, but the only person I knew how to be."

I wiped away one of her tears and she turned her face toward mine.

"I never even liked any of those guys," she admitted. "I only took their interest because I could. Because it made sure I stayed at the top. If I wasn't at the top, I wouldn't know how to be anywhere else."

"I knew the girl you were before you were at the top," I told her.

She made a sound. "You didn't stick around for her."

I drew back, surprised. "What?"

She glanced up at the surprise in my tone. "You stopped coming over. You stopped calling to hang out. When I saw you in school, you would go the other way. I asked my mom about you, more than once. She always just said to give you time. Eventually I stopped asking."

"You think I blew you off?" I echoed.

"Well didn't you?" she demanded. "Or is that somehow my fault too?"

I never really thought about it from her point of view. It was just one day we were friends and the next my world fell apart. I did stop coming over, I stopped wanting to hang out. Being around Kelly and her perfect family was too hard.

By the time I was a little older, a little more on solid ground, it was too late.

She had new friends. Better friends.

"I tried to sit with you one day at lunch, a long time ago," I said, thinking back to that day in fourth grade. "I came over to your table and you looked at me like I was a stranger. Like you didn't even know me."

"I remember," she whispered. "I didn't know you anymore. That was years later. You hurt me."

I guess I did.

All these years I blamed her for changing, but I had changed too. I might even have changed first.

"My parents got divorced," I said, as a bitter taste filled my mouth.

"I know. My mom told me one of the times I asked about you. She said you needed time. I waited, but eventually I realized you weren't coming back."

I nodded. "She tell you anything else?"

Thunder rolled over head and she glanced up and then back at me. "No."

I nodded. "Your mom is a good lady. I can see why she kept it all to herself."

"What?"

"The gossip. The truth."

She just stared at me waiting, like she had in fact been waiting for an explanation, even after all these years.

"My father had an affair with his receptionist. My mother found out when she took him a surprise lunch to his office and found them…" I cleared my throat. "On his desk."

Kelly gasped. "No!"

I nodded. "He'd been seeing her a while. The baseball games he missed, the dinners. He even missed my birthday party,"

"I remember that," she murmured.

"He was with her."

"I had no idea."

"No one did except some of the people at the dealership. But it was swept under the rug because he's so successful. No one wanted to talk against him."

"So they covered it up."

"Pretty much. And my mom suffered for it."

"You did too,"

Her soft reply pierced my chest and I pushed on. "He left us. He walked out and married his secretary. He left mom with the house mainly because I think he knew people would talk if he didn't. Mom never said anything all these years because she didn't want gossip going around; she was trying to protect me."

"But the damage was already done."

It's like she knew. She knew how I felt without me having to say it.

"People had to have talked…" she murmured trying to work it out in her mind.

"They did. But not for very long. He moved across town with his new wife and eventually people forgot."

"You don't ever see him?" she asked.

I shook my head. "The other day in the kitchen, when I was on the phone?"

She nodded.

"I called him to ask for money for the plumbing repairs. It was more than Mom can afford, and she was talking about getting another job."

"Eric," Kelly said softly, and put her hand over mine.

I pulled back though. I didn't want her pity.

"That was the first time I'd talked to him in over a year."

"Guess that explains why you were so upset."

"I shouldn't have taken it out on you," I apologized.

"Are you kidding? I deserved a lot worse than that."

I half smiled. "Yeah, you kinda do."

"You weren't supposed to agree." She poked me in the middle.

I laughed.

"That's why I stopped coming around," I admitted. "When he left, it was hard. I didn't take it very well."

"That's understandable."

"I stopped playing baseball. I didn't want to go anywhere, or be friends with anyone. I was just so mad at him. At night I could hear my mom crying in her room. She thought I couldn't hear. I still haven't told her I could."

This time when she reached for my hand I didn't pull away.

"That had to have been a terrible time for you and your mom. I wish I'd known. I know we were just kids, but I'd have tried to help."

I nodded. She would have. I knew it then and I knew it now. "It was too hard to be around you. I was so mad, mad at the world. I was mad you had a mom and a dad who loved you. Your dad is great, Kel. He'd never turn his back on you."

"So you stopped wanting to hang out."

It was like it was all clicking into place.

"It went on for a while, over a year. But my mom started worrying. She didn't cry about Dad anymore, but about me. I saw it when she looked at me. So I started studying more, getting good grades. I met my best friend, Ryan at a science camp I went to over the summer, then the next year we were in the same class."

"Is he the one with the suspenders?" she asked.

I laughed. "Yeah. He thinks they look good."

"I'm sure he's very nice, but suspenders just aren't for anyone."

"Why don't you tell him that?"

"Maybe I will." She smiled.

I grinned. Ryan would crap his pants if Kelly Ross talked to him. He'd die if he knew I was with her right now and I was staying at her house.

"Anyway, I really liked science. It made me feel like I was in control of something, you know? Equations and elements. Everything had a reason and a logical answer. It made more sense to me than all the other stuff, you know?"

She nodded. "Makes sense."

"I didn't realize you thought I blew you off." I felt kind of dumb for not seeing it until now. I'd been so caught up in myself and what was happening at home.

"I understand now. You probably thought the same thing that day at lunch."

"You had new friends, cooler ones. I thought I embarrassed you."

"Maybe you did," she whispered. "I was hurt. I thought I did something wrong to make you go away. So I made new friends. When you came over that day, people laughed. So I laughed too. I was afraid they'd laugh at me if I didn't."

"We grew apart," I mused.

"In different directions," she added.

More thunder rolled and the rain was unrelenting.

I held out my hand to her. "What do you say we get out of here before this shack falls over?"

"In the rain?" her eyes rounded.

"I don't think it's letting up anytime soon," I pointed out.

She seemed unconvinced.

"C'mon, it will be like all those times we used to play in the rain."

Kelly slid her hand into mine and allowed me to pull her to her feet. We stood there for long seconds in the dark, staring into one another's eyes.

She was still there. The girl who'd been my best friend.

Deep down, she was there.

The more things change the more they stay the same.

The meaning of that statement was suddenly clear. It was there, in the depths of Kelly's eyes.

Circumstances change, people change with them. Everything around us has the ability to change. But who we are, at our very core… it doesn't.

Who we are as people – on the most basic of level – it doesn't change.

And at Kelly's most basic level was a good person. A good friend. A daughter loved by her parents. She was afraid of the dark.

She was who I wanted.

Even back then when I was barely seven years old, I knew.

My most basic level knew Kelly was the one.

Maybe that was why I spent so many years being angry at her for changing.

I changed too, though.

But we were both still here all along.

"You ready for this?" I asked, grabbing hold of the door.

"I think so," she replied.

I couldn't help but feel like we were talking about more than the rain.

The second we stepped out, we were drenched beneath the downpour. Kelly shrieked and pulled my jacket around her.

My hand gripped hers tighter because the water made her skin slick as we dashed across the grass.

"Agh!" Kelly yelled and our hands were yanked apart.

I glanced behind me at her figure sprawled out on the grass. She had slipped and fell.

I rushed back to her side as she pushed herself up. Her front was entirely covered in mud and grass.

"Damn heels!" she cried and pulled them off her feet and threw them beside her.

I grinned so hard water ran into my mouth.

She glowered at me. "It's not funny!"

It was totally funny. She looked ridiculous with her make-up smeared, her hair plastered to her head, and mud and grass streaked all over her.

I held out my hand to help her up and she took it.

But instead of pulling her up, she pulled me down.

I landed in a heap right beside her, my white t-shirt instantly filthy.

"Hey!" I roared.

She laughed. A real, genuine laugh, and I tackled her, pressing her into the soaked ground with my weight.

"Eric!" she screeched. "Ew!" she pushed at my shoulders but I wasn't going anywhere until I wanted to.

I pushed up just enough so I could look down at her beneath me.

Something in the air changed around us and our smiles faded away.

My entire body was soaked as rain tried to drown us. But I was already drowning in her eyes.

Water dripped off my nose and chin, the drops falling down onto her as I swiped at the wetness and the streaks of make-up on her cheeks.

"I must look a mess," she said.

"You look beautiful," I replied.

She felt perfect under me, her body pressed against mine. I wanted to taste her again, to press my lips upon hers once more.

A bolt of lightning lit up the dark and she jumped. "We should go!"

Reluctantly, I got up and pulled her to her feet. She gathered her muddy heels and held them against her chest as we dashed through the yard and onto the sidewalk. As we ran she fished the keys out of her purse and tossed them to me.

"You drive!"

The car came into sight and I gave a shout of relief. I rushed to open the passenger side door, and the key slipped the first time as I shoved it in the lock.

"Wait!" she yelled as I held the door open for her to jump inside.

"What the hell are you doing?" I yelled over the rain.

Kelly was staring past me and the car down the street. "This is Todd's car!"

"So?" I said, not bothering to look where she pointed.

"So, he tried to punch you."

"Tried is the optimal word here," I said. I knew how to defend myself. I didn't just take science, I also took some boxing classes.

"He insulted you!"

"Who cares!" I gestured for the car.

"Me!" She took the door and slammed it shut and took off in the direction of his car.

I ran after her, giving up all hope of getting dry any time soon.

She stopped beside a red Mazda RX-7 and then glanced all around.

"C'mon!" I yelled at her, wondering what the hell she planned to do.

"Do you see anyone around?" she asked.

Alarmed I glanced around. "No."

She ran over to the opposite side of the sidewalk and picked up a large rock. It was big enough that her fingers didn't wrap all the way around it.

Before I could say anything she ran over and bashed it into his headlight, which shattered instantly.

She looked up at me as the glass fell onto the road and grinned.

I couldn't help but smile.

She looked ridiculous and wild just then.

I held out my hand and she reached for mine. A few steps toward our car she yanked free and threw the rock. It hit the passenger side window and sent a huge crack right up the center.

"Hurry up!" I yelled, wanting to get out of here now more than ever. The last thing we needed was to get caught.

Seconds later, we were in the car and heading toward her house. Both of us were soaked through, full of mud and grinning ear to ear.

"What the hell was that?" I asked.

"That was me doing what I should have done the minute he called you a charity case."

I chuckled and focused on the road.

"You aren't, you know that right?" she said a few minutes later, I felt her eyes on me.

I glanced over quickly. "What?"

"A charity case. You aren't. You're actually a really great guy."

"You should let people see this side of you more often," I said.

"You mean the side of me that vandalizes jerk's cars?" she giggled.

I smiled. "No. the side of you I've always known. The one who cares about more than being popular."

"I'm not sure if people would like that me," she confided.

"I am, because she's pretty great."

I wished Kelly could see herself as I did tonight. She was more real right now that she'd been to me in years. Even more real than when I kissed her under the stars.

Man, I wanted to kiss her now.

If she could, then she'd see. Kelly didn't have to be who she thought everyone wanted, all she had to be was herself.

Chapter THIRTEEN

Terms *used when dating:*
1st base – Kiss with tongue. **2nd base** – Felt up,
Fingered Handjob.
3rd base – Oral sex. **Home run** – Intercourse.

Kelly

MY DAD'S CAR WAS STILL GONE, which meant we were home alone. Eric parked in the driveway and we ran around the back of the house to enter through the back door that opened into the mudroom.

Both of us were so wet we were dripping, and I knew if we dragged mud all over the floors my mom would have a cow.

We were both laughing as we stumbled into the house.

"I wish we could see his face when he sees his car!" I laughed.

Okay, so maybe bashing in his headlight and breaking his window wasn't the most mature thing in the world. I didn't care. It sure felt good.

"That'll ruin his high," Eric scoffed.

"He is totally high all the time," I agreed.

I moved to shut the door and lock it behind us when I noticed all the muddy footprints we were getting all over the floor.

"We can't go through the house like this! Mom will kill me."

I grabbed an old towel off a stack of rags and started wiping up the mess. Then I tossed another towel to Eric and used one to wipe off my muddy feet. "Clean up," I instructed.

"This towel is just not big enough to clean up my entire body," he joked.

I frowned as my towel dangled from my fingertips. Water was dripping down my leg and my shirt was plastered to my body. He was right.

I glanced at the washing machine and knew what I had to do. I lifted the top and tossed the dirty towel in I used to clean up the floors. "Throw your clothes in there. I'll wash them."

After the towel, I tossed his jacket in.

"What about yours?" he asked.

"I'll wash mine too." I reached for the bottom of my shirt, then froze. He was staring at me. The way his eyes looked made me feel flushed. "Turn around!" I demanded.

He spun instantly and I stood there to make sure he wasn't going to peek back around.

Quickly I pulled off my skirt and belt and threw it all in the machine. My panties were soaked but I left them on, well, because.

I glanced up at the thought and my breath caught. He'd taken off his shirt and by the way his arms were moving I could tell he was unbuckling his pants.

He had a nice back. It was broad and smooth. His curls were soaked and his hair plastered to the back of his neck.

I tore my eyes away and focused on my top and bra. Once they were both in with the rest, I grabbed a towel out of the small linen closet and wrapped it around my body. On impulse, I pulled the scrunchie out of my ruined hair and tossed it in too. I ran my fingers through my ends to get the worst of the tangles out, and when I was done it hung in damp strands down my back.

"Done?" Eric asked.

"Uh, yeah," I said.

He turned around. His eyes swept over my towel covered body and my fingers tightened on the top as I held it in place. All he was wearing was boxers. I mean, it covered just as much as a bathing suit, but still...

It was so intimate.

I couldn't help but stare at him. He was so... pleasing to the eye.

I don't know how long I stared at him, feeling the spark of desire low in my belly before he spoke up.

"Should I turn this on?" he asked, stepping toward the washing machine.

I jumped, almost like I'd been caught, and busied myself with the laundry. Once the machine was filling with water and our shoes were by the door, I stared at him again.

The whole time I moved around I'd felt his eyes. Just the heat of his gaze was enough to keep me from getting cold.

"How late do you think our parents will be?" he asked, and his eyes swept down my towel covered body.

I shivered.

"I'm not sure. Could be a while."

"We should probably go change then, just in case they come back early," he replied, his voice low.

His hair was wild and no longer wet, but damp. He must have rubbed the towel over it while I was changing. He wasn't wearing his glasses either, something I'd barely noticed until just this second. His bare shoulders and arms had been too much of a distraction.

I nodded, but made no attempt to leave the small room. "Where are your glasses?"

He held up his hand where they were enclosed in his fingers. "They were wet, so I took them off to dry, didn't bother putting them back on."

"Can you see?" I asked.

He smiled. "All the important stuff."

Was it just me or did his voice get a little husky with those words?

"You look different without them," I said.

"Good different or bad different?"

"I like the way you look both ways." I glanced away shyly. He made me feel vulnerable, but in a good way. I was used to vulnerability as feeling like a weakness.

But this.

This vulnerability was different. It was sort of like opening myself up, allowing him to see past the walls I put up as a boundary. I felt exposed with Eric, and not because I was standing here in a towel.

I wasn't on guard with him constantly.

I realized I trusted him.

"Wanna hold my hand?" he asked, reaching out.

"What?"

He chuckled. "To walk upstairs. It's dark in here. Unless you plan on turning on the lights as we go."

I'd rather hold his hand.

We walked together up the stairs, hand in hand, with my other clutching the towel around me. There was a small light on in the kitchen, but the further up the stairs we got the less light it provided.

It was still raining cats and dogs outside, and thunder still shook the sky occasionally. "I had no idea it was supposed to storm tonight," I murmured, listening to it beat against the windows.

"Good night to watch a scary movie," he mused.

"You like scary movies?" I asked, remembering what he said before.

"Love em. Do you?"

"They're okay," I said. Since I was afraid of the dark, scary movies weren't really my thing.

He chuckled like he knew I'd been lying.

As we passed by the bathroom, lightning flashed through the sky in a sudden bolt. The bathroom lit up like a firework because of the skylight in the ceiling and then a loud boom of thunder ripped through the night.

I shrieked and leapt forward against him. His arms closed around me instantly and my cheek hit his bare chest. Without thought, my arms went around him.

His skin was warm and inviting. I'd never felt so invited to be this close to anyone. It was almost like he'd been waiting for me to jump at him, almost as if he wished for it.

The second I moved he was there, scooping me close and holding me tight.

The towel wrapped around my body fell loose when I put my arms around him. I didn't realize it until I shifted closer and my nipples hardened.

A lot of my skin was touching his and my body was reacting. It was rare for me to react so strongly to a guy. I'd been out with more than a few... but only one other one before Eric had made me feel desire.

And it wasn't like this.

The towel was still enough to keep us from being totally skin to skin, still between my breasts and him, but all it would take was one step. One movement and it would fall to the floor.

"You okay?" he asked, his voice next to my ear. My eyes closed at the sound of his voice. It, coupled with his arms around me, was overwhelming. Behind the towel my nipples tingled and I was starting to think all the dampness in my panties was not from the rain.

"Kel?" he asked when I didn't answer. He pulled back just enough so he could look down at my face.

The towel slid a little more.

I sucked in a breath as one nipple grazed his chest.

Quickly, I looked up, wondering if he noticed, if he felt it too.

His stare was heavy lidded, his eyes almost closed. His mouth was pulled into almost a grimace.

"I'm sorry," I said, totally thinking that he was turned off. "I didn't mean to jump at you like that and the towel... I'm sorry." As I rushed out the words I pulled back and grasped for the fabric, but it fell to the floor at my feet.

I crammed both my arms over my chest for some attempt at

modesty, which was really pretty pathetic. I hurried to bend down to fetch the towel but his hand on my shoulder stopped me.

"I liked it."

I paused and glanced up.

"You really thought I wouldn't?"

"Your face just now…" I trailed away, straightening but keeping my arms over me.

I felt his stare all the way to the balls of my feet. In fact, my toes curled into the carpet as he looked. Slowly, he reached up and grasped both my arms and tugged.

"Let me look."

The blatant request caught me off guard and set my blood to buzzing. I let him pull away my arms and direct them to my sides.

He made that grimace face again, this time, he growled with it. "You're so perfect."

"You think so?" I asked, thinking of how small my chest was and that most guys preferred more.

"Do you know how hard it's been to lay right across the hall from you? To walk by the shower sometimes and hear it running, knowing that you're in there naked?"

"I've listened for you," I admitted. "Wondered what you were doing, too."

Eric's fingertips brushed over my shoulder and trailed down my arm. "Can I touch you, Kel?"

"Please," I whispered. At that moment I wanted nothing more.

His fingers left my arm and dragged across my abdomen to circle around my belly button. Lightly he dragged upward, feathering a touch over my ribs. I closed my eyes anticipating him going higher, waiting…

His entire palm settled over my breast and I sighed. He kneaded gently, lightly caressing the hardened bud in the center. When he was done with one he moved to the other and did the same.

I gripped his sides and held on as he touched and caressed me.

When both his hands settled on both my breasts I made a sound.

Barely a second ticked by and his hands were sliding across my jaw and he was cupping my face and lowering his mouth.

His kiss was just like before, commanding and smooth. His lips moved with expert care over mine, drawing out a whole host of feelings and raging desire.

As I swayed toward him, his hands left my face and I was encompassed against his chest. My chin turned up and his mouth slanted over mine with a ferocity I thought only existed in movies.

Boldly, his tongue stroked along mine and delved deep into my mouth. I tried to kiss him back with equal fervor but the truth was, Eric was slaying me. Like, making it impossible to think, or breathe or concentrate.

As we kissed, his fingertips floated along the length of my spine and flirted with the waistband of my panties.

My hands slid up his back, my nails scraping lightly against his flexing muscle and it only turned me on more.

He was turned on too, I felt the evidence of his desire pressing against my belly. The length of him seemed impressive and every so often it would jerk slightly against me.

Another low rumble of thunder overhead seemed to wake him up. His mouth tore free of mine and our eyes collided.

"Are you a virgin, Kelly?" he asked, his voice was so gravelly I barely recognized it.

"No," I said. "There was this one guy,"

He shook his head once in a definitive slashing motion. "I don't want to hear about it. It will only make me crazy."

"It wasn't—"

"No." He shook me gently to get my attention. "Not another word about it."

I didn't want to talk about Brandon anyway. He was the only guy I'd ever actually liked that I went after. Sure, it started as just a game, but then I got to know him a little bit. He made me laugh and the whole mismatched sock thing totally charmed me. For the first time in forever I'd thought I'd found a guy I didn't want to chew up and spit out. I slept with him. And then he broke it off.

At the time I'd been hurt. I'd assumed he was just one of those guys who only wanted one thing and once he got it, the girl didn't matter. I'd been embarrassed to be duped by him. I should have known better. I should have seen right through his game... after all, I played that game all the time.

At least I never let it get as far as sex.

So there I'd been. I lost my virginity to a guy who didn't care. I knew by the look on his face after we'd done it (the second time) and he was casually putting his clothes back on, I'd done the wrong thing. I was still scrambling out of the bed when he dumped me.

The big jerk couldn't even have let me get dressed first.

He planned on telling everyone about this. About how he hit a home run with Kelly Ross and then dashed all the hearts and stars in her eyes. I'd wanted to cry.

I didn't.

I swore if he told anyone he was the one who ended it, I would tell everyone at school his penis was so tiny I wouldn't sleep with him and that's why he dumped me.

He was a jerk. We'd only had sex twice, and both times were nothing like the girls in the locker room said it was like.

Really, Brandon just taught me the way I played guys was the way to do it. Use them and then lose them as soon as I could. Before they hurt me first.

Too bad it took the guy I gave my virginity to teach me that lesson. All the other guys I had only kissed and made out with. A couple, I'd let go to third base, but Brandon was the only one who I went all the way with.

Until now. Until Eric.

I really wanted to go all the way with him.

"Are you?" I asked, curious.

He smiled. "No."

I don't know why but this surprised me, but the surprise was quickly squished by jealousy. I didn't like the thought of him having sex with anyone else. "Who!" I demanded.

His smile was wolfish and it totally transformed his face. "Are you jealous?"

Heat curled low in my belly and between my legs began to throb. His large hands spanned the sides of my waist as he started walking forward, pushing me backward.

"No," I said as his teeth latched onto my earlobe. I gasped.

"No?" he licked across and sucked it between his lips. My back hit his bedroom door and I arched into him.

"Maybe," I relented.

He laughed low in my ear and pulled back.

Both his hands came up to rest on either side of my head. "No one you know," he murmured and went for my lips again.

I turned my head. "Then, where...?"

He kissed my cheek instead and trailed down to my neck as he spoke. "Summer camp isn't just for textbook learning and science experiments, you know."

I grabbed a handful of his hair and pulled his face up. His eyes widened a little, but a smile pulled at his mouth. "I don't want to hear anymore, either."

"She wasn't near as beautiful as you," he whispered. "I want you, Kelly."

His hips thrust forward and his rigid length rubbed against my middle. Just feeling it... I knew what I'd said to Brandon hadn't even been a lie. His penis was totally small compared to what I was feeling right now. Must be why my threat to tell worked so well.

Can't fight the truth.

"Do you have protection?" I asked, running my hands across his chest.

"In my room." He reached down and turned the handle. Before shoving open the door his arm slipped around my waist so he could support my body.

We started kissing again as he backed me into the bedroom. I heard the sound of the door closing but I barely registered it. I was falling down a black hole of desire, where the only thing that existed was his body and mine.

I strained to get closer, even though we were pressed together tightly.

His hands cupped my ass and kneaded the flesh, making me purr.

The back of my knees hit the bed and buckled. We fell back onto the mattress with him on top. His weight was delicious, and I rubbed myself against him like a cat.

He whispered my name when his lips left mine and my head fell to the side when his mouth closed over my breast.

"*Oh,*" I moaned, and he sucked a little deeper.

He played and sucked until I grew impatient and grabbed his hair once more. His throaty chuckle was almost my undoing and I spread my legs and tried to pull him up my body.

"Hang on," he said and left me. I heard him rummage through the bag and I reached down to pull my panties off.

"I got that," he said, coming back and stripping the cotton down my legs and throwing them away. I sat up and reached for his boxers, helped him pull them down.

His cock sprung out instantly and I stared. It was long and thick, and he was so hard the skin was taunt. I reached toward it.

Before grasping him, I looked up and he nodded.

I stroked and explored him, reveling in the strength and softness of it. I stroked him a few times, enjoying the way his body seemed to hum, until he reached down and pulled my hand away.

He climbed on the bed between my legs and ripped open the packet.

I stared at his body while he worked as my stomach quivered with nerves and my body shook with need.

Before climbing over me I felt his hand brush my thigh. "You're shaking."

"That's how much I want you," I said honestly.

"I'll stop," he told me.

I covered his hand with mine. "Please, don't."

His hand pulled from beneath mine and moved to my center. My eyes went wide when he brushed at the wetness. Brandon had never done that. He never touched me there.

Eric's other hand pushed my thigh out wide, so I was more open to him.

His name formed on my lips and it was like he heard before I spoke.

"Do you trust me, Kelly?"

"Yes," I replied without hesitation.

I was slick, dripping with desire, and his fingers spread the silky liquid around further, swirling it around the most sensitive spot on me. He plucked gently at my swollen bud until I moaned and writhed against the bed.

Tension built up inside me so strong I felt like I might explode.

When he left the spot I exhaled with slight relief only to have his finger penetrate my body. The pad of his finger rubbed against my inner walls and my eyes rolled back in my head. God, this felt good.

He felt good.

"Eric," I panted when that pressure began building up inside me again.

His hands left me entirely and his body settled over mine. He braced his weight on his elbows and pressed our lips together.

At the same time, he entered me in one long stroke. I called out but he swallowed the sound and began to move.

I loved the way he didn't hesitate; he was sure in his movement. His surety made me enjoy it more because it inspired confidence. And because he really knew how to move.

His cock totally filled me up and stretched me out. My inner walls vibrated with pleasure and with every thrust, he went just a little bit deeper.

I wrapped my legs around his waist and his forehead dropped onto my shoulder as he thrust into me again and again.

And then he hit this *spot*. A magical spot that caused an explosion inside me. My teeth sank into his shoulder and he continued to ride me hard.

I came with so much force I ceased to hear and see. When at last my body let reality back in, my legs slid from around him like melting snow and I collapsed into the bed, a boneless, satisfied mess.

"You still with me, Kel?" he whispered, rising up over me, balanced on his hands.

I smiled.

His movements quickened and his breathing turned shallow. I felt his release inside me and I heard it in the air when he moaned.

When it was over, he rolled to the side and pulled me with him so I was lying half across his chest. I could hear his heart beat right beneath my ear.

I thought it might be my new favorite sound.

Well, okay, maybe it was tied with his voice.

His fingers toyed with the ends of my hair and dragged up and down my spine. I laid there in the afterglow, my body completely relaxed and my mind only in the present.

For a little while anyway.

"Sounds like the rain is letting up," Eric whispered.

I made a sound of agreement.

"Kel?" he whispered again.

"Hmm?"

"Was that okay for you?"

Ah, for once, some vulnerability in his voice. It was almost as endearing as his floppy curls.

I smiled against his chest. I thought about teasing him, but I couldn't bring myself to do it.

I lifted my chin and propped it up on the back of my hand and looked at him. "It was better than okay."

His teeth flashed white in the dark and he rolled so he could kiss me.

"I gotta go clean up," he said, pushing off me. "Before they get home."

"Kay," I replied, watching him.

Before leaving the room, he turned on a small lamp over on the dresser and then lifted it down onto the floor so it wasn't so bright.

"Cause I won't be able to hold your hand in the dark while I'm gone," he said, bestowing upon me an adorable yet sexy smile.

When he was gone, my mind started to wonder. I thought about the party and my horrible nickname. I thought about the way everyone teased Eric and called him a geek.

I thought about Mandy and what a horrible friend I was.

I was at odds with everyone, including myself.

Eric let himself back in the room and slid on a pair of boxers. Next, he tossed me a t-shirt, one of his.

I slipped it on and as he laid back down, he pulled me close.

I guess right now I wasn't at odds with Eric.

But the longer I laid there and thought, the more it became clear. Something was going to have to give.

I could reclaim my status. Tonight was awful, but it wasn't something I couldn't overcome.

Did I want it back? Was being at the top, being a *man-eater* really worth the cost?

I felt the softness of Eric's lips at my hairline and I smiled. The smile quickly faded away though when sadness overcame me.

The cost of that life—of popularity—was suddenly very high.

I couldn't have both, of that much I was certain.

I was going to have to choose.

Popularity or Eric.

Chapter FOURTEEN

Crunchy – to be jealous.

Eric

~~Girls like Kelly are dangerous.~~

Scratch that.

I've never met anyone like Kelly before.

I will rephrase.

Kelly is dangerous.

Dangerous because she has the ability to walk off with my heart.

The ability to hurt me.

I wasn't in love with Kelly. Right now, I was in serious like and lust. It wasn't as if we'd just met. Yes, we'd been best friends a whole other lifetime ago.

But as I'd been discovering, the kids who we were at our core was still the same back then. Did that mean I knew her, at least in some sense?

In the most important sense?

It was like we were reconnecting, but doing so in a different way.

I'd opened up to her in the fort. I told her things I hadn't even told Ryan. She'd told me how she thought I basically abandoned our friendship. I guess in some ways I had.

And then she did that day at lunch when I tried to sit with her.

I never tried after that and neither did she.

We settled into co-existing in the same school, but in completely different realms.

I couldn't even be mad at her anymore about the way she behaved. I understood it now. I might not agree with how she's handled her friends and popularity, but who was I to judge? We all handled things differently.

I got the distinct impression she wasn't happy. She didn't really like who she pretended to be. I hoped after the night we had and the way we talked, she'd realize she didn't have to pretend.

I thought things might be different.

She slept with me most the night after we'd had sex. The second we heard the front door open and close, she'd rushed into her room and several minutes later I heard her talking to her mom in the hall about changing her mind about staying at Mandy's.

I also heard her tell my mom I'd gone to bed hours ago and was likely asleep.

After the house settled down and all was quiet, I'd gotten up and crept to the door. Slowly, I pulled open my door and peeked out to realize she was doing the same.

Her smile was brilliant and she raced across the hall and into my room. She was still wearing my t-shirt; it was just covered up by a robe.

We spent the rest of the night making out and sleeping. Kelly didn't go back to her room until the sun began to rise.

I'd had sex with two girls before her. I could honestly say, Kelly was the best I'd ever had.

I already wanted her again.

I loved the way her body responded to my hands. The way her legs quivered when I was between them. The sounds she made drove me wild and the surprise in her eyes when I did something that truly pleased her made me feel like I was riding on a cloud.

I didn't see her much the next day because she went out with her mother and we went by our house to see how the work was progressing.

Looked like things were on track and we would be going home very soon.

Mom was of course mad I'd called Dad for the money. She scolded me, but not very much. Deep down, I knew she was relieved and that was enough for me to take her lecture.

I'd asked for too much apparently, so with the rest I told her to buy herself something nice. She deserved it.

We smiled at each other during dinner and I waited for her to come to my room that night.

She didn't.

I went to my door twice, thinking I'd go to her, but something held me back.

Something close to fear.

Now that the weekend was over and she'd had time to think... did she regret the night we spent together?

Was she sorry she slept with me? Did it change nothing at all?

The next morning at school I found out.

She ignored me completely.

It was like a kick right to my balls. I watched her covertly every time I got the chance. Most people treated her like they always had, like she was the most popular girl in school.

I did see Rebecca giving her some dirty looks, but Kelly seemed to be unconcerned. There was a definite strain between Mandy and Kelly, and I'ad stayed far away from them both.

I wondered if she apologized to Mandy and if things were on the mend between them.

I hoped so. I wouldn't want a friendship she'd had for many years to fall apart.

At the end of the day I couldn't take it anymore. I was pissed off she was ignoring despite me several attempts to make eye contact.

I walked right up to her locker where she stood with several of her friends. Everyone fell silent, meaning not just the people beside her, but in the entire hall.

"Hey, Kel," I said, forcing the words out and to sound normal. "Can we talk a second?"

You could have heard a pin drop as I waited for her reply.

All eyes turned to Kelly, but her eyes stayed on mine. I saw her answer in the blue depths before she even spoke. She quietly begged me to understand, she silently whispered and apology.

"I'm busy right now," she said.

"Seriously?" I said, anger making me hot.

"Get lost, geek," one of the other girls said, stepping in front of Kelly.

"I'm not a geek," I said, my voice hard and cold. The eyes of the girls eyes who were standing around went wide. They expected me to just rush away. "Being a geek implies I'm really smart, but as it turns out, I'm pretty stupid."

"Eric," Kelly said softly, and the girl in front of her turned to stare. It wasn't her way of apologizing—it was just another plea for me to understand.

But I didn't.

I never would.

I walked away and didn't look back.

That night, Mom and I packed our stuff and went back home.

I'd thought maybe things would be different.

But the more they changed, the more they stayed the same.

Chapter FIFTEEN

Buggin' – when you are worried about something.

Kelly

IT WAS JUST LIKE ALL THOSE YEARS AGO.
Eric approached me at school and everyone started to laugh.

I turned him away.

I was too afraid they'd laugh at me, afraid they'd turn their backs for good.

It was the worst thing I'd ever done. Worse than stealing boyfriends, and stringing them along. Even worse than that time in third grade when I pretended not to know him.

This time, I knew all the facts, I understood how we grew apart and I'd been there when we fell back together.

I turned my back in spite of that.

I regretted it the instant he walked away.

What was the point in being popular if you were that way for all the wrong reasons? What was the point of being popular if getting that way earned you a horrible nickname?

I glanced around my locker after Eric disappeared and I realized something.

I didn't like any of these people.

I didn't trust them.

So why did I care?

Was I so worried someone might not like who I was, that I totally went against everything and hurt the person I liked most?

I couldn't do it.

I wouldn't turn my back on Eric a second time. I wanted a friendship with him. I wanted a relationship.

I wanted a man who was solely mine. Not because I flirted and manipulated. Not because I stole him away. I didn't want to "chew him up and spit him out."

I just wanted to be happy.

Eric made me happy.

After school, I went to Mandy's. I had some major making up to do. Out of everyone she was the one friend I wanted to keep. She was someone I actually liked. I was ashamed of myself for acting the way I had with Tad and I was glad he told her the truth.

I said all of that. Every bit. And then I told her about Eric.

By the time I left her place, it was almost dinner and she and I were on our way to a real friendship, not one that was just based on social status.

The second I walked in the front door, I looked for Eric.

I raced into the kitchen expecting to find him waiting for dinner, but no one was there but Mom.

He'd gone home. Packed up and left.

I raced up to my room and dialed his phone number. Even after all these years I still knew it by heart.

His mom answered. She told me he wasn't home.

I knew it was a lie.

I'd screwed up. I screwed up so bad I was terrified I'd never be able to fix it.

Eric wasn't like Mandy. I couldn't have a girl heart to heart while we did each other's hair and be besties again.

He'd opened up to me, basically laid it all on the line. We spent a night together I would never ever forget.

Then I threw it in his face.

It couldn't be too late. There had to be something I could do. It couldn't just be words and promises. He wouldn't believe me. He'd think the second things got tough I'd turn on him again.

I couldn't even blame him.

I'd have to show him. I'd prove he meant more to me than every ounce of popularity I had.

It was going to have to be something big.

A grand gesture.

I just hoped I wasn't too late.

Chapter SIXTEEN

Gag Me with a Spoon – a way to say you are disgusted by something or someone.

Eric

Two days later…

THE BEAKER IN FRONT of me bubbled up with bright blue liquid and I knew immediately I'd screwed up. I watched with boredom as it bubbled up and spilled over the sides and rushed down onto the table.

The white foam spread out around the glass and I just watched.

"What the hell is wrong with you?" Ryan exclaimed grabbing a handful of brown paper towels to start cleaning up my mess. "This is a basic formula! You could do this in your sleep."

"Too bad I wasn't sleeping," I retorted mildly.

His eyes about fell out of his head.

"All right," he said, tossing down the towels and running his hands along the elastic bands of his suspenders. "That's it. You've been acting like you're on drugs for almost a week now."

I rolled my eyes and he leaned close.

"Are you on drugs?"

You know your life has officially become a shit circus when your best friend literally thinks you're on drugs.

And when you mess up a totally basic chemistry lab.

Mr. Brawn approached the table with a displeased look on his face. "Is there a problem here, gentlemen?"

"No, sir," Ryan hurried to say. "We just mixed up a couple elements."

"Clean it up and do it again. Right this time."

"Of course," Ryan agreed and picked up the paper towels again.

When Mr. Brawn was back at his desk, Ry looked at me. "Well?"

"No, I am not on drugs."

"Then what is it? Your mom get a boyfriend? Did you get a boyfriend?"

"For someone so smart you sure do say some wacked out shit," I muttered.

"Girl trouble?" he guessed.

I glanced away.

"Holy crap, that's it," he whispered like he was in awe I would have any kind of relationship with a girl that would constitute "trouble."

I ignored him and cleaned up the mess I'd made and carried the ruined beaker to the sink to trade it out for a clean one so we could start over.

"I want to know everything," he demanded.

"No," I said.

"You can't say no. I haven't had any action… like… well, ever, so I have to live vicariously through you."

I couldn't help it. I smiled.

He thought that meant I was going to spill my guts. I didn't want to talk about Kelly. It still stung too bad. It still hurt.

Ever since we moved home I'd been in a permanently distracted and foul mood.

Mom even tried to talk to me about it and I bit her head off. I knew she knew it had to do with Kelly. Hell, she wasn't blind.

But I refused to talk about it. Period.

"You wouldn't believe me if I told you," I told Ryan.

"Is this about the party over the weekend?"

I glanced at him, my mouth agape.

"What? I hear stuff too."

I laughed.

"So you and Kelly… is that just a rumor?"

"Hey, you hear that?" the girl at the table beside us asked her lab partner.

Just about the same time I heard the muffled sound of music in the distance.

Everyone in the room started looking around, trying to figure out where it was coming from. A couple people went to the windows and a few pressed their faces to the windows on the classroom door.

"Calm down, everyone," Mr. Brawn said.

No one listened.

The music started to grow louder. As in whoever had it playing must be busting an eardrum because I could hear every word of the song.

It was by The Police. "Every Breath You Take."

"Hey look!" someone said, and pointed through the glass in the door. The entire class crowded around and started talking all at once.

Over the announcement speakers came an announcement.

Music is not allowed in school. Whoever is playing it needs to shut it down immediately or they will be given detention.

The music didn't stop. It seemed to get louder.

"She's just standing there," a student said loudly. "She's looking right at us!"

"Okay, step aside," Mr. Brawn said and went to open the door.

He reared back as soon as he did because the music was just that much louder.

"Ms. Ross," he yelled into the hallway. "What on earth are you doing?"

"It's Kelly Ross!" someone else said excitedly.

My stomach dropped just hearing her name. I sat down at my seat and pretended not to hear the music or the commotion.

Ryan looked at me like I grew an extra head, and took off.

Everyone was talking now. And singing along. I heard doors out in the hallway open up and people begin to crowd the hall.

About a minute later Ryan came back. "Uh, man. I think it's for you."

I jerked up. "What?"

"Go look."

"No."

"Dude, if you don't go look out in the hallway right now I might start doing drugs."

I rolled my eyes. He grabbed the back of my shirt and dragged me off my seat.

"Fine," I muttered and went to the door. Only problem was, there was a crowd of people standing around.

I shoved my way through only to be met with even more of a crowd. People were laughing and staring, they were whispering.

"Turn that off right now!" Mr. Brawn yelled.

I glanced ahead of the crowd and saw what looked like the top of a boom box.

I shoved through the crowd, and suddenly it gave way to a large open circle where everyone gathered around and pressed into the hallway.

In the center, standing between people and lockers, was Kelly.

She was dressed in Jordache jeans, converse sneakers and a bright pink top.

But it wasn't what she was wearing that got my attention. It was what she was doing.

She was holding up a gigantic boom box over her head as it played the song.

When she saw me she smiled.

"What the hell are you doing?" I yelled over the music.

"Waiting for you!" she yelled back.

The crowd was getting larger, even the teachers were watching with interest, no one even tried to break up whatever madness she was doing.

The song went off and the PLAY button on the boom box popped out.

Everyone waited.

I waited.

She sat the box aside and motioned for me to step forward. When I didn't, she came to me and grabbed my hands.

"I was a total idiot. I got caught up in all this stuff that didn't matter. In popularity. I should have done this the other day at my locker, but I was scared."

People were whispered, some laughed. She didn't seem to notice. It was like we were the only two people in the room.

"You are the most genuine person I've ever known. You don't take any of my crap and you don't care about my status. You were my very first friend, even before we knew what the meaning of friendship really was."

"What are you saying, Kelly?" I asked.

"I'm saying I want that back. I want to be friends. But more than that, I want to be more than friends. You're the first guy in this entire school who's ever stopped me in my tracks and made me think about who I am as a person."

"Man-eater," someone yelled from the back of the crowd.

"Yeah, maybe that is what I was. But not anymore! I don't have to steal boyfriends, or play games just to keep my status. Real friends wouldn't care who I like or what my hobbies are. Or even the way I dressed." She glanced at Ryan and I was pretty sure he peed in his pants a little.

"That's me!" he called out. "She meant me!"

People laughed.

"Dork!"

"No!" Kelly cried. "No more names, no more labels. Ryan isn't a dork because he wears suspenders and Eric isn't a geek because he likes science."

My heart swelled and I tried not to give in. I tried not to fall just a little bit more.

"I'm telling the entire school, right now, that I, Kelly Ross, am totally into Eric Seaver. I like his glasses, his messy hair and his love of science. And if anyone has a problem with that then they can bite me!"

"Language," Mr. Brawn scolded.

Kelly grinned and squeezed my hands, but there was a question in her eyes.

I hesitated.

Kelly let go and turned away. My stomach fell. But she didn't go far, she hit pulled out the cassette tape, flipped it over and put it back into the boom box.

The second she hit play, the same song by The Police started playing again. She lifted the box above her head and stood there.

She looked ridiculous.

It was pretty damn irresistible.

I walked into the circle, her eyes never left me. "What are you doing, Kel?" I asked.

"I'm standing here like this until you agree to give me another chance."

"That boom box is awful heavy."

"Don't you see? You belong to me," Kelly said.

"Wow. That was cheesy," I teased.

"I'll start singing. All the lyrics. Every. Last. One."

"Kiss her already!" Mandy yelled. I hadn't even noticed her on the edge of the crowd.

I looked back at Kelly.

She nodded.

I set the boom box aside, but let the music play.

"I think I'm falling in love with you," she told me.

Right there in front of half the school.

"What do I gotta do to get you all the way to love?" I asked.

"Kiss me."

"Okay," I agreed. "But this time I'm not going to let you go."

"I'm counting on it."

She was laughing when I pulled her into my chest and pressed my lips to hers.

We were still kissing when the song ended.

We were still kissing when everyone was ordered back to class.

Kelly Ross was my friend before we even knew was friendship was. She was my change that remained the same. She was my hardest goodbye and me sweetest hello.

She was my first love.

My last love.

And everything in between.

About Cambria Hebert

- *Cambria was born in 1981* -

Cambria Hebert is an award winning, bestselling novelist of more than twenty books. She went to college for a bachelor's degree, couldn't pick a major, and ended up with a degree in cosmetology. So rest assured her characters will always have good hair.

Besides writing, Cambria loves a caramel latte, staying up late, sleeping in, and watching movies. She considers math human torture and has an irrational fear of chickens (yes, chickens). You can often find her running on the treadmill (she'd rather be eating a donut), painting her toenails (because she bites her fingernails), or walking her chorkie (the real boss of the house).

Cambria has written within the young adult and new adult genres, penning many paranormal and contemporary titles. Her favorite genre to read and write is romantic suspense. A few of her most recognized titles are: *The Hashtag Series, Text, Torch,* and *Tattoo.*

Cambria Hebert owns and operates Cambria Hebert Books, LLC.

You can find out more about Cambria and her titles by visiting her website: http://www.cambriahebert.com.
Email: cambriahebert@rocketmail.com
Facebook: http://smarturl.co/CambriaHebertFanpage
Twitter: https://twitter.com/cambriahebert
Pinterest: https://pinterest.com/cambriahebert/pins/
GoodReads: http://www.goodreads.com/author/show/5298677.
Cambria_Hebert

www.ingramcontent.com/pod-product-compliance
Lightning Source LLC
Chambersburg PA
CBHW070554180626
46817CB00005B/1838